TABLE

ML NYSTROM

————— HOT TREE PUBLISHING —————

For information, contact the publisher, Hot Tree Publishing.
WWW.HOTTREEPUBLISHING.COM

EDITING: HOT TREE EDITING
COVER DESIGNER: CLAIRE SMITH
FORMATTING: RMGraphX

ISBN: 978-1-925853-35-3

DRAGON RUNNERS MC SERIES:

MUTE
STUD
BLUE
TABLE

This book is dedicated to survivors. You know who you are. Peace and strength be with you always.

And to Brittany Alexander for all her support and encouragement along this amazing journey.

CHAPTER 1

I snapped the last towel in front of me and smelled the fresh laundry scent wafting up from the thick cotton. I quickly folded it and tucked it onto the shelf in the huge linen closet, taking care that all the stacked towels were folded the same way and lined up perfectly. The owner of the house was very vocal on how she wanted things to be done and how they should look. The last time I worked in this house, she was put out because the linens were put up "sloppily" and she liked "clean, straight lines" when she opened her closets and cupboards. I just nodded and said, "Yes, ma'am," but fumed at the pettiness. Currently, the woman was down by the crystal-clear pool giving the evil eye to the pool man who painstakingly maintained it. I guess she really had nothing better to do than incessantly pick over petty details.

I took one last look at the immaculate towels and closed the folding door. The rest of the massive bathroom sparkled, the odor of cleaners gone and only a hint of freshener lingering in the air. Hopefully the lady of the house would finally be impressed during her "inspection." I gathered the last of the cleaning supplies and left, careful not to leave any footprints or marks of my presence behind. The master bedroom was elaborate with dark, heavy furniture, and the hall to the ornate sweeping staircase was filled with expensive-looking antiques. I was being extra careful not to touch anything. Not all the homes in this million-dollar neighborhood of Biltmore Forest screamed ostentatious, but this one did. I spotted Maria working at the counter in the state-of-the-art kitchen.

"All done, eh, Lori?" she asked as she wiped her hands clean from the vegetables she had been preparing. Maria was the housekeeper and cook for this wealthy family, but the gigantic house was more than she could keep up by herself. The Hispanic woman had to hire extra hands weekly and paid in cash since the turnover was so high. I'd been here three times already, but I had a feeling this would be the last. Most of the housekeepers in this elite neighborhood who hired extra hands paid in cash, and I'd gotten work from several of them over the last two weeks since I got stuck in this town. One only had to go to the local coffee shop to pick up the quick cash jobs from the notices tacked to the board inside.

Maria glanced through the large kitchen window at the lounging mistress of the house and frowned. She pulled an envelope of money from her pocket and handed me my day's wages. "If I need you again, I'll call you."

"Thanks, Maria. And thanks again for the referrals." I took the sealed envelope and tucked it into the back pocket of my worn-out jeans. Just by the look on her face, she wouldn't be calling again. Some of the rich here were good people, and others were flat-out snobs. Maria worked for the latter, and the owner wasn't satisfied last time with my towel-folding abilities.

The older woman pursed her lips. "My cousin, Constanza, has a cleaning service and is always looking for good help." She held out a slip of paper with a phone number written on it. "I told her about you, so if you call, just tell her I sent you."

I thanked her and then went out to the ancient GMC Safari I had recently purchased. It was made sometime in the 1980s, had balding tires and a transmission that was going bad, but it still ran well enough to get me from place to place, and the owner was fine with a cash sale. My last car had also been old and cheap, and had died a slow death. It had finally given up the ghost and left me stranded in the North Carolina mountain city of Asheville. I was forced to dip into my money stash to buy another one. The sale had to be under the table—no dealerships, no bank financing, no papers—so my only option was Craigslist and someone willing to take cash. If I was ever pulled over by the police or involved in a wreck, I was screwed. Buying the minivan meant I had to stay in the area for a while, working the cash jobs to replenish my depleted funds before traveling again. I'd been up and down the east coast for the better part of a year, doing nothing more than surviving. If I could hang on just a few more months, and if all went according to plan, I should be free and clear. My traveling would be over and I could finally settle somewhere and get my life back.

I tore open one end of the envelope and pulled out eighty dollars. No tip, of course. It's amazing that some people who have such riches at their feet are so tightfisted, and other people who barely had enough themselves would share whatever they had in a heartbeat. I tucked the money into the hoard of bills I kept in the side pocket of one of my backpacks and mentally tallied them up. At this rate, I may have to spend the rest of the fall around Asheville, working wherever I could as long as it paid in cash.

There were worse places than this beautiful, eclectic city. The scenery itself was breathtaking, and it was almost a requirement to stop and look at the colors of the surrounding mountains. Asheville had a lot of support for local businesses and artists. There was a plethora of homegrown produce in the farmers' markets, many microbreweries, and a huge variety of handcrafted items from local artisans. There were street musicians busking around the downtown square, colorful sculptures, and other quirky bits I found appealing. I'd explored a bit when I ended up here a couple of weeks ago and was able to fit right in with the folks who lived here, making enough contacts to find the type of work I needed to get. Yes, there were worse places for me to end up.

I'd been spending the nights in different places, sometimes a discount motel room, sometimes in my van at a campground, and sometimes just wherever I could park safely. If I was going to stick around, I needed to find something cheap and longer term, but no lease. Hotels were out. Tourist season was year-round, so the prices were too high even at the really shady places. I drove to the library and used their free computers to do searches for month-to-month room rentals in the local papers as well as Craigslist.

An hour later my eyes were starting to cross. There were plenty of rooms available but not nearly as cheaply as I hoped. The ones in my price range were still way higher than I was willing or able to pay and still be able to replenish my funds. One ad finally caught my eye.

Room for rent: Above detached garage. Private bath, separate entrance. Some furniture but no phone, no cable. Rent is 400.00 a month, cash money or taken in trade with work around the house and yard. Might need some heavy lifting and running errands. Prefer a single female. No parties. No drugs. No drinking. Serious inquiries only.

A barter system? That could be a really sweet deal, but it really depended on the work that was required. I scribbled down the number and went to get a coffee at a nearby coffee place. I winced a little at the price. Almost three dollars for a simple black coffee? I was really getting bad about pinching pennies until they screamed in agony.

After getting my coffee, I sat down and pulled out my phone. The woman that answered the phone sounded nice but in a no-nonsense kind of way.

"This's Martha. What can I do ya' for?"

My cheap Tracphone crackled a bit, and the sound was faint, but it still worked well enough.

"Hello, ma'am. My name is… uh… Lori Matthews, and I'm interested in the room you have. I'm a hard worker, and I don't party at all. I'm mainly interested in what kind of bartered work you're wanting?"

"We need someone to do some light housework 'n some yard work and some gardenin' work. Maybe some babysittin' sometimes. My grandson does most of the heavy stuff, mowin' the grass and trimmin', but he don't do no flowers or the daily gardenin'. He works nights mostly, so's me 'n my sister takes care of his baby girl when he's out 'n we could use some extra hands."

Housework wasn't a problem and neither was gardening. I wasn't too sure about childcare, but beggars can't be choosers. This sounded like the break I was hoping for and I needed to jump on this offer quick.

"No problems with anything. May I come by and look at the room sometime soon?"

"I got a man coming later tonight to look but I'd'ruther have a woman here. You got time to come see it now?"

Her thick Southern drawl was hard to understand as she rattled off the address. I managed to get directions and found myself driving to a secluded area in Woodfin, just north of Asheville. Without a GPS, I had to rely on verbal directions from the barista and Martha. "Jus'bout a mile past the big crooked tree that overhangs the road, you'll make a right on the gravel road afore you get to the lake" were apparently acceptable Southern guidelines for directions to finding this cheap room.

Somehow, I managed to find the place.

It was perfect! Hidden at the end of the gravel road and surrounded by tall trees was a plain ranch-style house with several storage sheds, a barn, and a two-car garage with the promised room above it. I noticed a chicken coop next to the garage with a number of the birds strutting and pecking the ground. Behind the structure was a fairly wide creek that burbled along, probably one of the tributaries of the French Broad River that was fairly close by.

The woman who answered the door look like a wizened elf. Her body was tiny and wiry and her face was covered in wrinkles. She wore pink capris and a bright yellow flowery shirt. A wide straw hat with fake daisies on it crowned her head, and gardening gloves were on her hands.

"You the woman that called me 'bout the room?" she asked.

"Yes, I'm Lori Matthews. Nice to meet you." I reached out my hand for her to shake.

She took one glove off and pumped my hand twice. I was surprised at the strength.

"Nice ta meetcha too." She turned and yelled into the house, "Carol! Tenant's here! I'm heading over!" She closed the door abruptly before the other occupant could answer. "Daylight's a'burnin'. Come on up to the garage and see the room."

She strode off briskly toward the back building. "There's steps. A mite steep but ain't too bad. Iffen I can handle 'em, Imma sure you can."

There was an outside staircase that *was* rather steep leading up to the room. The door was unlocked, and Martha simply opened it and tromped inside, her work boots echoing in the space. It was one big room, with a queen-size bed on one side, an old box TV on the other, and an area set out to be a kitchenette. There was a small bathroom with a shower stall, sink, and toilet. It was very plain but functional and just what I was looking for.

"Ain't much to look at, but it's clean. Ain't got no cable TV. Got satellite for the big house and maybe can run you a line out here iffen you want it, but you'll hafta pay the extra," Martha informed me as I looked around, walking on the worn '70s green shag carpet. There was a bit of a musty smell, but nothing I couldn't stand for a short period of time. The way my life was now, I just needed a place to crash between jobs, not a home. Someday, I hoped I would have a home again.

"Before you say anythin' bout the room, lemme show you the garden. That's the main help we need." She tromped back outside, grunting and leaning heavily on the railing next to the steps. "I don't get around like I used to and watching my great-granddaughter takes a mite outta me. My sister's up at the big house too, but she's older 'n me. Garden path's over yonder." She pointed to a bridge leading across the creek. "You drive an ATV? That's what it takes to get there now. I used to walk it every day, but my knees is gettin' bad. Come on."

She opened the garage doors, revealing two four-wheelers, one of them with a giant barrow behind it, and a variety of other gardening equipment. She gestured at one and expertly mounted the other. I'd never driven one of these before, but it couldn't be too hard, right?

I stalled it twice before I was able to get it going over the bridge. I followed Martha up a well-worn incline path, through a thick tree line to a long, open clearing. I was stunned by what met my eyes.

When she said garden, I was thinking a few plants, bulbs, and flower beds to maintain. This was a field full of green rows of vegetables. I saw hills of yellow squash and zucchini, racks of pole bean vines, rows of tomato cages, lines of corn stalks, and other vegetables I couldn't identify by sight. It was overwhelming, and I could see why these ladies would be interested in trading help to maintain this monstrosity.

"Been growing a garden all my life. Puttin' up beans 'n' maters 'n' such, selling down to the farmers market over at the college. My last tenant was a man, but he didn't last too long. Said I done worked him too hard 'n he couldn't keep up." She sniffed and peered at me with her piercing eyes. "You think you can? Rent is four hunerd dollars a month, but iffen you'll help out, say around ten hours a week, I'll give you the room an' some board for half. If it turns out ya work more 'n ten hours, I'll knock off an extra hunerd or so."

Two-hundred-dollar rent or less just for helping work a garden? I would've been stupid to turn that down. "Yes, ma'am, I can keep up, no problem."

Martha grunted. "Got daylight left. Might as well get started. I needs them yella squash plants harvested some. 'Bout done for the season. You can take a couple for your supper t'night. Bags are in the back of the ATV. When you got 'em filled, come up to the big house an' I'll show you where the root cellar is. Mind fillin' out a contract?

Name and numbers 'n such. I ain't gonna file nothin' 'cause it costs to make a record down to city hall an' I think it's a waste a' time, but we got a tenant a while back that took some stuff and we didn't have no way of findin' him. He was 'bout as sorry as you can get. My grandson insists on it, but he don't have a say in who I let stay here. It's one of them just-in-case papers. It keeps him happy 'n outta my hair."

I hesitated before I answered. I wouldn't be here long enough for it to matter. "Sure, I can sign a contract."

She climbed back on the squat vehicle and started the chugging motor. I watched as she left the area without a backward glance.

I stood for a moment, listening to the fading motor. Just like that, I had a place to live that I could afford. I turned to the bright green garden and got to work.

* * *

Later that evening, I moved my stuff from my van to my new room. It wasn't much, as I mostly only had minimal clothing and a few odds and ends from my previous life. The tiny kitchenette didn't have much in the way of cooking implements, but I had a few pots and pans and enough supplies to plainly fry the few squash and zucchini I'd picked earlier. I mentally added a trip to the grocery store sometime tomorrow to get a few more things, as cooking would be much cheaper than eating out all the time. Peanut butter was a great traveling food to keep on hand, but there was only so much of it I could stand.

As I was bringing up the last load, Martha came by with a key.

"Don't rightly have a call for such way out here, but I figured you'd want to lock up. Need you to gather the eggs tomorrow morning out the coop and bring 'em up at the big house. You done good with the squash. Need to get the 'maters tomorrow morning. Might need to thin out the turnips later this week. Taters are almost ready, too. My boy'll get them in with the backhoe soon as the tops get browner. Here's the contract. See you in the mornin'."

The woman turned and went back down the steps, again without looking back. I didn't know who decided older southern women were supposed to be gently sweet and demure. Martha was as hard and dry as the gravel in her driveway and seemed to be just as tough. The contract she handed me could barely be called one. It was nothing more than a piece of torn out notebook paper with the word contract handwritten at the top and lines on it asking for name and social security number. Not even an official signature. Just name and numbers.

I called Constanza Velasquez about doing some house cleaning work for her, and she had responded with an enthusiastic "yes-when-can-you-start?" I had gardening work in the morning and house cleaning in the afternoon, and whatever else I needed to do at this farm in the evening. With any luck, I could keep that kind of schedule and be able to get my finances back to a healthy place in no time. Then I could get back on the road and keep moving. Just a few more months was all I needed.

It was deep into the night when I bolted up from the nightmare, gasping and gagging. I threw the worn comforter off my sweaty body, not wanting anything touching me, and jumped out of bed. The room was dark except for the dim reflection of the outside dusk-to-dawn pole light that lit up the backyard. I heard nothing but the burbling of the river and the night bugs singing a low chorus of buzzes and chirps. My breath slowed down as the quiet peace of this place settled around me. I was in an isolated part of an isolated town, on an isolated mountain, living with isolated people. There was safety here.

A faint throbbing growl from a vehicle caught my attention. It was getting louder and closer, and my heart seized up at the unexpected sound. *No,* was my first thought as the panic climbed up my throat. I rushed to the window where I had lowered and shuttered the blinds earlier and slipped one of the blades up to see what was happening. A dark male figure was riding a motorcycle into the yard, pulling in next to my van, out of sight of the house. Both man and machine were huge and menacing, but I sighed in relief. This had to be Martha's grandson coming home from his night job, whatever that was. A red Camaro convertible followed him and parked opposite the motorcycle and my van. The biker got off his bike and strode to the blonde woman emerging from the car. I watched as he gestured to my van and pointed to my room, shaking his head. I could faintly hear the woman's laugh but didn't hear her response. I watched as she shimmied back on the hood of her car, pulling her skirt up and spreading her legs wide. The biker took off his helmet, and I saw his head was completely bald, before it disappeared between the woman's legs. I heard her squeal and saw her lie back on the hood, one hand balancing on the car and one hand grasping the back of the man's head as he went down on her. He dropped his helmet in the grass and grabbed her hips, holding her still for his marauding mouth.

I wanted badly to look away, but I was mesmerized. The sounds of her pleasure were harsh and foreign to my ears. It had been a long time since I had enjoyed sex. A very long time, and I was feeling something I'd never thought I'd feel again just watching the raw carnality in front of me. My sex pulsed as if waking up from a long sleep.

The woman keened and grabbed the man by his ears as she came, looking like she would tear them from his head. He pulled her hands off him and anchored them at her hips, still going at her as she spasmed, her head thrashing against the car's hood. I held my breath, but it didn't look like she was fighting. It looked like she was digging in for more and the man was obliging her. She was making a lot of noise, and I glanced at the dark windows of the "big house," wondering if the elderly women inside would be awakened. He finally raised his head and stood back between the woman's spread legs, opening his black jeans, pulling out his cock. He took a few seconds to sheathe himself in a condom before pushing himself into the woman's body. She gasped and grabbed for him again, but he held her down as he pounded inside her. He was brutal, slamming into her over and over again, and she seemed to relish every moment. She came again, screaming out her pleasure. It looked rough and wild, and I should have been appalled, but I wasn't. The man thrust into the woman one last time as he threw his head back, and his low grunts reached my ears. He wasn't as noisy as the woman, but the way he slumped over her body meant he'd found his satisfaction too. She ran her hands over his shining head and said something to him. They laughed and shared a moment before he pulled out of her. He took care of the condom and tucked himself in his jeans as she scooted off the hood of the car and righted her tight skirt. She went to hug him, and he squeezed her back, giving her a quick peck on the top of her blonde head. They had a few more minutes of muted conversation before she climbed into her car and left. He stood in the low light watching her leave and then turned and went into the house.

I was wide awake now and buzzing from the show. Part of me was turned on and wanted to do something about it. Another part of me wanted to run like hell, leave everything I had and just escape.

I did neither.

I climbed back into bed and tears gathered in my eyes as I rolled over, curling into myself. Someday soon, I'd be free of my demons. At least I hoped so.

***

Table watched as Lottie drove away. It had been just a few months since he had moved back to the farm, but this was the first night in a long while that he had been able to go out and be an adult. Money was tight and time was tighter, so he would take advantage of any chance he could to get a moment of privacy. Work at the tattoo parlor was going well, his grandmother's garden was growing huge, and his baby daughter was thriving despite being abandoned by her mother. After Lottie's headlights disappeared, Table glanced at the dilapidated van parked in the side lot next to the garage. Martha had mentioned looking for a tenant and helper for around the farm. He thought the offer was more than generous and hoped this new guy would work out. The last one put the *L* in lazy and Martha soon overworked him. Table wasn't thrilled with the idea that some random stranger would be living with his grandmother and her sister, but he knew that anyone who didn't measure up would soon be out on their ass, and for the time being, he would be there to help enforce Martha's farm rules. He looked briefly at the dark window of the rental room before moving to the house and entering. There were four bedrooms in the ranch-style house, all of them small but at least private, or private enough. Both Martha and Carol's doors were cracked slightly, but Angel's was all the way open. Table quietly moved through the tiny room to the crib that held his world. The tiny girl was curled up, her puffy diapered bottom in the air. Her face made a few movements as he stroked a finger over the velvet softness of her young skin. He had never expected to be a father until that fateful night when his life turned on itself like a mountain road switchback. His wife, now ex-wife, had shown up out of the blue at his favorite bar while he had been on a date with a woman he was interested in getting to know better. Tamara had set the baby in the carrier on the pool table along with a bag that held a few supplies in it and walked out the door, leaving Table to cope. One look at the pink bundle that was his flesh and blood was all it took for the future to turn in the most unexpected direction. Table decided then and there that he had to move back to Asheville and the farm, both for help with his new fatherhood role and to figure out his next plans. He had thought he would be moving back permanently, taking up the farm as his inheritance and raising his daughter as he had been raised, but he found himself missing the mountains of Bryson City and the club family he'd left behind.

Angel grunted and shifted in her sleep. Table smiled at the squirming bundle. No need to make earth-shattering decisions tonight. His divorce had been finalized that afternoon and he had gotten laid in celebration with a good friend from his past. Life would work itself out. He left the sleeping child and went to find his own bed, content for now.

CHAPTER 2

The sun had risen, and the river sparkled with the morning light as I made my way down the steep stairs. *Gathering eggs?* I'd never gathered an egg that wasn't already in a cardboard carton, but really, how hard could it be? I found out this morning when I ventured into the spacious chicken coop. Hens of all colors were flocking around a long row of nesting boxes that were full of different shades of brown eggs. They cackled and clucked as they milled around randomly. I went down the line, trying not to think about the chicken poop I might be walking on and picking up the warm orbs, until I came eye to eye with a red and orange hen sitting on a nest. She looked at me and cocked her head to one side, sizing me up. I swallowed, as I'd never been this close to a chicken that hadn't been plated on a dining room table. The wicker basket was almost full, but I still needed to get the eggs that may still be in that nest.

"Shoo!" I spat, trying to sound authoritative. The bird opened her beak and snapped it shut in a clicking sound.

I tried again, this time with a hand motion. The hen just settled herself even further into the nest. I put the basket down and clapped at the cantankerous animal. All I got was a baleful glare.

I was being intimidated by a damn chicken! I shook my head. This was a bird not exactly known for its intelligence level. I reached into the box, fully intending on slipping my hand under the bird to at least feel for any eggs. What I got was a lesson on how angry a chicken can get and the sharpness of its beak. It jumped at me with a loud squawk and pecked at me several times before I could yank back my hand. Then it came running at me and leaping at my legs. I yelped and fell back on my butt in the dirt, narrowly missing the basket as I tried to get away from the enraged fowl. The bird clucked at me and raised its head in triumph as it strutted off to a different part of the coop. My hand was burning and bleeding from several deep puncture wounds, and the worst part of the whole encounter? There weren't any frickin' eggs sitting in the nest!

There were three short steps framed by a wooden railing to the back door. I knocked on the screen door, holding the basket awkwardly as I cradled my hand at my middle, trying to staunch the bleeding. I was expecting Martha or her sister to open the door, thinking they would be the only ones up at this hour. Instead, I got my second shock of the morning.

The bald biker from the previous night answered the knock. He was tall, broad, and shirtless, showing off an incredibly colorful array of intricate tattoos on his defined arms and chest. The details were astounding. I forced myself to look up at his face and not at the gold loops decorating his dark nipples. The color of his hair, if he ever let it grow in, would be a dark, deep brown going by the neatly groomed Fu Manchu mustache and chin duster that framed his mouth. There was a touch of gray, indicating some maturity. He was big all over, his stomach and shoulders showing clear and precise delineations that could only come from a lot of physical work. Power exuded from every pore, and I found it both intriguing and intimidating. I should have been scared, but I wasn't.

Why?

Because he had a tiny baby dressed in pale pink cradled in the crook of his hard bicep. He held her close, curling her securely into his body, protecting her. How could anyone be scared of a hard, strong man who was cradling a baby like she was the most precious person in his world? It was enough for me to relax. Right?

His deep brown eyes regarded me silently, and I held up the basket.

"I have the eggs." My voice came out croaky as my dry tongue stuck to the roof of my mouth.

His mouth split into a grin that showed off the whitest teeth I'd ever seen. I could see his natural charm, the kind that was irresistible. One look at that devastating smile and women would be lining up. My lower stomach tingled as I remembered him burying his head between the woman's legs and her reaction.

He turned his head and yelled back in the house, "Yo, Nanny! Your tenant's here with the eggs!"

"Imma comin'!" I heard faintly from the interior.

The baby squirmed in his arm and let out a little grunt. He jostled the pink bundle and made shushing noises at her. "Ch-ch-ch almost there, baby girl. Almost there."

He looked at me and smiled again. "Bottle's not quite ready and she can get impatient. Name's Table."

Table? Strange name for a girl, but the last year had been a strange one for me in a lot of ways.

"Never knew a little girl named for a piece of furniture."

If I hadn't been holding the heavy egg basket with both hands, I would have slapped one over my mouth. I didn't want to anger my landlady and that probably should extend to her grandson.

He seemed to take my faux pas in stride and laughed, those beautiful teeth flashing again. "Nah, *my* name's Table."

"Nice to meet you, Table. I'm, uh, Lori."

His smile got bigger and he nodded at the fussing baby. "This is my little girl, Angel. Come on in to the kitchen. Nanny's gonna have food ready soon and I'll bet money she's got a full plate with your name on it."

I entered the house like I was stepping back in time. The furniture was old, antiques you'd see in a museum-type house, but the pieces were still being used regularly and looked well cared for. I caught a faint scent of bacon grease in the air and heard the pop and sizzle of cooking meat. The kitchen contrasted with the antique look of the furniture. It was huge, with stainless steel modern appliances. Martha was shuffling around the stove, wearing another bright floral top, this time with blue denim capris. Her wiry gray hair stuck out and curled up into an odd-looking crown around her head.

"Jus' put the eggs on the counter," she ordered as she flipped the bacon.

Another elderly woman approached me. This must be the sister, Carol.

"Ooh my! Looks like the biddy hens worked some overtime last evening!" She clasped her hands in delight and giggled. "You must be the Miss Lori that Martha let the room out to. Nice to make your acquaintance, dear!" She reached out a hand and took mine in both of hers. "Looks like one of them gave you what for. Let's take care of those bites at the sink. I have some salve and some Band-Aids in the cabinet. We'll get you fixed right up!"

Carol looked and sounded the opposite of her sister. She wore a pale powder-blue house dress and beige orthopedic-style shoes, whereas the colors Martha wore were big and bold, and she was sporting bright orange Skechers.

Carol fussed over my hands and her blue eyes glowed as she patted my bandaged extremities. "There we go, all done. Tell me, child, are you saved?"

I faltered; I had no idea what she was talking about. Martha grunted and slammed a bowl down on the counter. Table burst into laughter, his head thrown back and mouth wide. Angel squirmed in his arm and made a few baby noises. A bottle was in his hand and he had plugged it into the baby's mouth. She was eagerly downing the contents, oblivious to her father's mirth. My stomach flipped again at the odd sight of the half-naked tattooed biker guy feeding a baby.

"Carol, I done told you not to try recruitin' for the church!" Martha stated as she pulled several white plates from a cupboard. "Not everyone goes to see the Good Lord on Sunday mornin' and they ain't all going to hell neither. Sit on down, girl."

It took a moment to realize she was talking to me. I was a little scared of the demanding woman, so I did as she ordered and sat at the round table.

Carol sniffed and went to get silverware out of a drawer. I had the feeling of becoming a rope in a tug of war between the two sisters. My face must have shown something, because Table stepped in.

"Stay here long enough, Lori, and Martha here will have you up at her secret still makin' 'shine by the end of the week. Carol will ask you next about singing in the choir Sunday morning. Don't pay any attention to them and they'll stop."

He lifted Angel to his cloth-covered shoulder and patted her back. She let out a loud burp and Table laughed again. "That's my girl!"

Martha scowled at him and plunked a plate in front of me, loaded with crispy bacon, three eggs fried in the grease, a pile of fluffy white grits covered with melting butter, and thick pieces of toast slathered with red strawberry jam. My eyes bugged out at the amount of food and I immediately calculated the amount of fat, carbs, and calories I was expected to consume.

"I didn't get t' show my still to that last tenant at all! Carol scared him off right quick with her hellfire and brimstone preachin' at the dinner table."

"I beg your pardon, sister! It was you scared him off with your talk about still flashfires, going blind from bad 'shine, and all that other nonsense! Plus you done worked him too hard!"

"Bah! That 'n was jus' too soft. He didn't like gettin' his hands dirty."

I just stared at the heaping plate in front of me. Martha put a larger one in front of Table and Carol brought two more, filling out the four places. Both sisters sat down and joined hands. Martha was to Table's left and I was to his right. She placed her hand on Angel's tiny one. Carol reached out her other hand and looked at me expectantly. Table did the same.

I felt a choking sensation crawl up the back of my throat. I took Carol's hand without a problem but I looked at Table's offered one and hesitated for an awkward moment. My eyes rose to his as the silence grew uncomfortable. I could see the question in his deep brown eyes.

"It's just saying grace, baby girl. The odd couple here kinda have a thing about it at meal times." His voice was velvety low and calming.

It was just a hand and there were other people in the room. I could do this. I held my breath as I reached the last few inches to slip my small hand into his large one. I felt the warmth from his palm as he lightly clasped my fingers. He winked at me and bowed his head. I barely heard Carol say the prayer, acutely aware of the man next to me. He wasn't holding me hard, but I felt every cell in my body focus on that one point of contact. He didn't make a big deal of it. He dropped my hand just after "amen" and started eating one-handed, still holding Angel over his shoulder.

The two sisters nattered on about the garden, farmers' market schedules, and other stuff. I started eating and somehow managed to clean off the plate. After breakfast, Carol took over the kitchen, clearing the table and loading the dishwasher. Table cooed at Angel as he disappeared into the back of the house, presumably to change the baby and put her down for a morning nap.

Martha got up and announced it was time to go pick tomatoes. "Daylight's burnin'. Time to get crackin'."

I followed her out to the garage and helped her load supplies and garden tools onto an ATV. I congratulated myself on getting through breakfast. Now it was time for me to earn my keep.

CHAPTER 3

I parked the ATV and pulled out the hoe, spade, and digging fork. It was late morning and Martha was at her house watching the baby and I was working in the garden solo for a bit. She wanted the soil turned around the tomato plants as well as some of the squash, zucchini, and other vegetables harvested for the North Asheville Farmers' Market held on the UNC-Asheville campus every weekend. I'd been here for two weeks and had learned a lot about the people I was essentially living with.

Martha was the younger of the two sisters and was bold and outspoken. She wore bright clashing colors always and was constantly moving, working either in the giant garden, the chicken coop, or the house. She didn't ask if you wanted anything to eat or drink, she just put it down in front of you and expected you to take it. Carol was sweetly southern and always wore some sort of pastel dress or skirt. Her standard answer to anything was to "pray about it."

I was expected to sit at the table every morning for

breakfast, but I was on my own in the afternoons and evenings. I was invited to dinner more than once and the one time I took them up on their offer, Martha greeted me at the back door with a cold beer from a local brewery while Carol scolded her for "encouragin' the consumption of spirits." I wasn't sure beer qualified as "spirits" but for Carol, it did.

I saw Table sometimes in the mornings, depending on his shifts at work. I found out he was a tattoo artist and worked part-time at a local tattoo parlor, mostly in the evenings, but occasionally he worked a day shift. I saw him more than once from a distance, cutting the enormous lawn area, fixing a loose gutter, under the hood of a car, and other maintenance jobs around the farm. Occasionally he joined Martha and me in the garden. Any free time he had, he spent with his daughter, caring for her, playing in the yard on a blanket, shaking rattles and cooing at her. I didn't see him with the blonde woman again. I was usually awake when he came home from a night shift, and I'd watch him pull into the parking area of the yard and go directly into the main house. This didn't mean he hadn't had any company, it just meant he wasn't bringing it home.

My life had become routine but tightly scheduled. I woke up early and worked the garden with Martha before the heat of the day settled in, then I spent the rest of the day working with Constanza at whatever house cleaning she had booked, and then either worked the garden again in the evenings or did other chores around the farm and house. Constanza was a beautiful Mexican-American woman, close to my age in her midthirties, single, with more energy and life than I ever hope to have. She'd named her cleaning business Hurricane Connie and it showed in her speed and thoroughness at each and every job. She didn't act like a boss and treated me as an equal even though she was paying me. My first job with her, she told me upfront to call her Connie and wanted to know when we were going out on the town. I still hadn't gone anywhere with her, but she was determined to be a friend. Truthfully, she was wearing me down, as I didn't have any real friends and could probably use one.

I pulled on work gloves as I knew I'd be pulling weeds and that could sometimes be tough. I'd already had several encounters that left my hands raw and bleeding; some of those grasses could be sharp as knives. I popped a wide-brimmed straw hat on my head to keep off the sun, loaded up my arms with the tools, and started walking through the tree line to the garden.

Promptly into an invisible spiderweb.

I screamed in panic as the sticky filaments covered my face and dropped everything as I swiped at the mess, hoping the web's occupant hadn't been hanging there in wait and was now somewhere on my body.

A roar of laughter finally caught my attention. Table was sitting on the big faded red tractor, a backhoe attached for the potato harvest, clutching his stomach and nearly falling off the machine. For a few minutes, he was incapable of speech.

"I—you—damn, baby girl!" He kept laughing and wiping at his eyes. "That was the funniest shit I've seen in a while."

It probably shouldn't have been that big of a deal, but watching his handsome face smiling wide with unbridled mirth did me in. Instead of joining in on the joke, I felt humiliated.

"I'm sure you've run into a spiderweb before. It's not that funny." Anger flared through me. He was making fun of me and I really didn't appreciate it. Right then, I hated him. "And I'm not your 'baby girl' or baby anything to you. I'm just the hired help for the season."

He kept laughing as he put the tractor in park and jumped down from the high perch. "Yeah, I've run into webs before. Easy to do here. Just never realized how fuckin' funny I looked while doin' the spider dance."

He slapped his arms around his body to demonstrate. He was wearing only a white tank and torn, dirty jeans but still looked hot.

I huffed and bent down, reaching for the stuff I had dropped. I could feel my face getting flushed and conflicting thoughts ran through my mind. I was mad and embarrassed but trying to convince myself he was really just joking. I wanted to laugh with him at my own expense and at the same time, I wanted to run away from him and hide. I was so distracted that when he crouched down next to me, I jumped back, falling on my butt in the process.

"Take it easy, Lori. I ain't gonna bite." He picked up a wide hoe and the basket of bags and shifted them to one hip. He rose above me, and I had to swallow the sudden intimidation I felt by his tall presence. His deep chocolate brown eyes regarded me before he reached out a hand to help me up. "Didn't mean to startle you. As far as the nickname, well, it's a habit, like callin' someone darlin' or sweetheart. I don't mean any offense."

I stared at the hand in front of me. My impulse was to take it, but my mouth got ahead of my brain. "I don't need your help," I spat, and shuffled off the ground, brushing dirt and debris from my worn jeans.

Table's thick brows came together. "What the hell? Did I do something to offend you?"

I knew his confusion was real, but I couldn't stop myself. Yes, I was mad and I didn't know why. Rage burned in my gut and I lashed out at him mainly because he was a handy target.

"I saw you banging a woman the first night I moved in and haven't seen her since."

He blinked and the look on his face changed from confused to angry. "Yeah, I was with Charlotte for a night. She was into it and I was into it. What's your problem?"

"A one-night stand, eh? Typical. She's probably one of a long line of women you use when needed and then discard when you're done."

"What the fuck?" He dropped the stuff in his hand to the ground. "First of all, lady, it ain't none of your business who I fuck, when I fuck, and why I fuck! My divorce was final that afternoon and Lottie wanted to help me celebrate. If you were watching the show, then you know I didn't force her to do anything she didn't want to do and I made damn sure she came, and came hard. More than once! I don't know what the fuck your problem is, but I suggest you get over it or put your ass in your van and get the hell out!"

My heart was pounding and I could feel my face drain of color at his anger. I managed to stem the flow from my mouth as Table stomped off and mounted the tractor. With an angry roar, the machine fired up and crawled back down the pathway to the main part of the property.

I released the breath I hadn't realized I'd been holding and nearly collapsed as my head spun. My hands and body were shaking and I wrapped an arm across my churning belly. I tried to control it, but it was too much. I bent over and vomited, retching and heaving. This was not the first time my mouth had gotten me into trouble. I really did have a good thing going here and was almost in the clear. I didn't need to mess this up any more than I already had. I needed to buck up and apologize and hopefully keep my place.

I managed to work through my panic attack with long hours of hard labor in the garden. The sun was bathing the sky in peaches and mauves when I caught Table as he was mounting his bike to go to work at the tattoo parlor.

"Table!" I called. Time to put on the big girl panties.

He looked up at me and scowled blackly but didn't say anything as I approached.

"Look, I'm sorry I lost my temper at you earlier today. I was embarrassed for you to see me run into the spiderweb and I thought maybe you were making fun of me. I lashed out. I know you weren't and I had no right to throw your private business in your face like that. Please accept my sincere apology."

He stared at me for a moment, his mouth turned down

in a frown. "How long did it take you to come up with that pretty speech?"

This was not going to be easy. "I'm— I don't have any close friends and I'm not very good at social cues. I take stuff too seriously sometimes and I shouldn't. It's my fault I overreacted and I'm really sorry for taking it out on you."

His face lightened up a bit. "Takes a strong person to admit when they're wrong. Apology accepted, but that don't mean I expect it to happen again." Table's demeanor was stiff, but at least he wasn't mad at me anymore. At least I hoped so.

"I'm sorry for goin' off on you so hard. It caught me wrong, but that's no excuse to talk to a woman that way. The better man in me would've just walked off. Let's just bury it and plant something on it. You take care of your business and I'll take care of mine. As long as you do right by the odd couple, I'm good with you staying here. Yeah?"

I took a breath to apologize again but managed to keep my mouth closed. Either I was forgiven or I wasn't and I absolutely was not going to beg for it. I gave him a little nod of agreement and then turned to go up to my room. I didn't look back when I heard his bike start up and he drove off.

* * *

Table pulled into the parking lot closest to Asheville Ink where he worked at night. His days were a combination of working around the farm as needed and spending time with his daughter, and nights were spent working at the tattoo parlor. He felt sleep deprived most of the time, but his time in the military had trained him to push through. Every once in a while, he was able to get a night out with the small Asheville chapter of the Dragon Runners MC, but this was rare. The members here were still brothers, but it wasn't the same as his home club in Bryson City. The local amateur boxing league wanted to see him return to the ring, but so far, he hadn't had the desire to try.

Lori was something he hadn't expected. For years, the little room over the garage had been "rented" to whichever cousin needed a temporary place to crash. He hadn't heard until he came home that his grandmother and great-aunt were now using the space for an income or bartered help. Table had made some calls and discovered the other grandchildren in the area hadn't known of this development either. It was not surprising that many people would take up an offer bartering work for rent, but farm work was hard and not many could handle it, especially with his grandmother's high standards. He hadn't realized how much help the two old women needed now and how dependent they were on other people. Still, his grandmother was always up at the butt crack of dawn, surly as hell and ready to work. Lori was up early as well. She had jumped in with both hands, never complaining and always getting the job done. Table had noticed she didn't sleep much more than he did, as her lights were usually on when he came home from his late work shifts.

Lori. Secret woman. Quiet. Kept to herself and then some. Table had asked his buddy, Blue, who was a deputy back in Bryson City to do a background check on the woman who was living with his two elderly relatives. Just as he'd suspected, the name and social security number listed on the handwritten contract were fake. Lori Matthews did not exist. Why he hadn't run her off yet was a mystery even to him, but there was something about those eyes of hers. Haunted was the word he used when thinking about her. The bad cut and dye job on her hair was clearly DIY and didn't suit her at all. She paid cash for everything, and while that kind of made sense since she was working cash jobs, he wondered if she had a bank account at all. Was she hoarding all her earnings in the room over the garage? Table had met people with wanderlust before, and he'd also met people who were just plain running from something. The latter tended to be quiet, kept to themselves, and stayed ready to move on at any moment. Like Lori.

But she worked hard at every task thrown at her by his grandma, completing it to the letter no matter how tough. He's been watching her closely and had never seen her drunk on the job, nor had he observed any signs of drug use. She had never brought home a man either. He couldn't judge anyone, as he himself had experienced some skirmishes with the law, both when he was in the military and when he got out. He had decided that as long as she continued to take care of his grandma's needs, she could stay.

However, her reaction this afternoon was telling. He'd gotten a glimpse into her brain when she burred up at him over his mirth at the spiderweb thing. Her fear in reaction to his anger and her clearly negative opinion of his night with Lottie didn't sit well with him. He didn't need her judging him. Moreover, something about her intrigued him. She was a tightly wound mystery behind thick walls, and even though she kept a serious lock on sharing anything about herself, his protective instincts were kicking in. His gut told him she needed help. He would do what he could and handle her with kid gloves for the moment; however, if he got even a hint that whatever troubles she might have would affect his family, she was out of there faster than a goose could shit.

CHAPTER 4

"What else do you have to do on a Saturday night? Wash your hair?" Connie snorted while wiping down the last kitchen counter. The odor of bleach wafted through the air.

"Yes, that's right, I'm washing my hair. All night." I rolled my eyes as I wrung out the rope mop, pressing hard on the squeezer handle of the bucket.

"Hmph." She sniffed again. "Your hair's too short to take all night. You should only take ten minutes or so in the shower, and most of that time is to shave your legs. Give me another ten minutes to touch up that nasty dye job and you'll be ready to go out tonight in no time at all."

I sighed. Connie had been after me for several weeks to go out on the town to one of her favorite hangout bars, called A.W. Shucks. She was also itching to get her hands on my hair and wardrobe, wanting to make me up like a living doll. So far I'd been able to put her off, but I was running out of excuses.

"Come on, *chica,* you're too young to hold up your life.

You gotta get out there and live a little!"

If only she knew.

She was looking at me with such pleading in her brown eyes, I finally acquiesced. "All right, I'll go out tonight."

Connie whooped and danced in a circle, waving her yellow-gloved hands in the air. "Yes, ma'am! You come to my house around seven. Anita and I will get you sorted. It's gonna be fun!"

That was how I found myself out with Connie and her sister, Anita, at a local bar. In the past, I'd been in some five-star hotel bars or ones with private club memberships, but I'd never been to a place like this. I'd always thought a bar was a small, dark place with a few tables and a long counter with slumped-over people drowning their lives in liquor. This place turned out to be so much more. It had at one time been a warehouse for a local cotton mill and had been converted into a bar that was more like a nightclub. The bar itself was in the middle, in a huge U-shape and surrounded at the top with flat-screen TVs showing every sports channel known to man. The sound was off and the stats were displayed at the bottom for people to read while drinking and listening to music. There were pool tables, darts, and other bar games, and local bands on Friday and Saturday nights.

And people. Lots of people. It seemed like the entire population of Asheville was there tonight. Some were dressed to impress, while others were more casual. There were couples and groups, and where some seemed to be focused on flirting or drinking, others looked to be there just to relax after a long work week or catch up with friends.

I hadn't really known what to expect when I drove up to Connie and Anita's house earlier, but I had a blast. It had been such a long time since I had fun while bonding with other women. Anita was a hairdresser and had taken one look at my head before sitting me down and bringing out her shears.

"Whoever's been chopping at your hair didn't do you any favors, *chica,*" she declared while combing and snipping. "The color is way too dark for your complexion. Damn, this stuff is thick! You should let it grow out some and give me more to work with."

I didn't tell her it was me who had been chopping at my hair.

When she showed me the results I was amazed at the difference she'd made. Just the light trimming of layers had shaped my ragged hair into a spiky pixie look that was both sophisticated and attractive. My eyes looked bigger and more open, and that combined with my height gave me a fairy-like appearance. Connie insisted I borrow her shiny teal cold-shoulder top and a pair of her heeled boots to give me some height. I wore the one pair of "nice" jeans I owned. I had to rein in Connie when it came to my makeup, as she was far more liberal with it than I wanted.

Anita opted to be the designated driver for the night and we crammed into her sporty red Mustang for the trip. Anita and Connie were apparently well-known, as the bouncer and many other people greeted them by name. In no time at all, I found myself with a beer bottle in my hand and surrounded by gyrating bodies on the dance floor. The band was good and loud, the music fast and hard-hitting. Connie waved her hands in the air and twisted, bumping her hip against mine. "Loosen up, Lori. We're here to par-tay!"

Despite myself, I did have fun, bumping and grinding, letting my guard down enough to enjoy not being alone. It had been such a long time since I'd danced and I wasn't sure if I'd ever let go enough in my life to move this much or this hard. Anita laughed and clinked her bottle against mine. Song after song blended together and we danced and danced and danced. A few men came around but all three of us managed to ignore them and they left us alone. Beer after beer found its way into my hand and down my throat and I could feel myself getting tipsy.

I noticed a group of men over at the pool tables engaged in a game. Four or five of them were wearing vests with the same logo on the back. It said Dragon Runners, with a fire-breathing green skeletal dragon that looked both majestic and menacing.

"Hey, do all those dragon people work for the same company?" I asked Anita as she hip bumped me. She laughed out loud and clinked her bottle to mine.

"Oh, girlfriend, you're such a tourist! Those guys own the place! It's a motorcycle group that rides around and shit. You're in the den of the dragon, baby!"

A motorcycle gang? A frisson of fear went down my spine. Motorcycle gangs were full of drug dealers and violent criminals, weren't they? Connie and Anita were laughing and dancing hard, not caring about the possibility of any danger. They were just dancing, drinking, and having a good time, so maybe this wasn't so bad. I'd met a lot of people who looked one way on the outside and were completely different on the inside. Judging a book by its cover was very often inaccurate. I could do this. I could keep dancing and having a good time, then head back to Anita's to get my van.

I tipped the bottle back and nearly choked when I spotted a familiar head over at the pool tables. He was bent over lining up a tricky shot. He stroked the cue stick smoothly through his fingers and tapped the white cue ball. The shot was good, and he moved around the table to the other side, giving me a clear look at the now-familiar logo on his back. Table was a Dragon Runner.

Table was a Dragon Runner!

The man I'd been working alongside and watched play with his baby daughter was a gang member. My heart stuttered and my brain went in a thousand directions all at once. We'd come to a truce since the morning I lost my temper at him. He did his work around the farm, I did mine, and we got along, even working side by side a few times.

He must have felt me staring, because he turned and looked directly at me. He blinked in surprise, then his face broke into a grin and he waved.

Instinct had me lifting my hand and waving back. Or was it the alcohol?

A loud crash sounded behind me and I whirled around. A man at the bar was gripping a waitress by her upper arms and screaming obscenities into her scared face. He was shaking and jerking her so hard, she could barely keep her balance. Broken glass and foamy beer was on the floor, telling the rest of the story.

"Stupid fucking bitch! Look what the fuck you did! Goddamn cunt! I ain't paying for that!" The man was obviously drunk, and violently so. The scene unfolded in front of me, almost in slow-motion. Droplets of spit flew from the man's mouth to land on the woman's face as she struggled to get away. She was crying, saying *I'm sorry, I'm sorry* over and over again, and trying to shrink into herself for protection, but there was none to be found. My heart raced and a sick sense of panic froze my feet to the floor. My head roared as all other sounds faded to nothing and my vision pinpointed, not on the furious man but on the woman. I wanted to move, to run away, but I was stuck, mired in my own fear.

My trance suddenly broke when a pool stick came down in front of the man's head and yanked back at his throat. The man released the woman and starting gagging and clutching at the stick that was forcing his chin up. She was quickly wrapped in the arms of a Dragon Runner and pulled away.

Table held the stick tight against the man's neck. The drunk's face was turning purple and his feet barely touched the ground as he arched to get away. Table didn't seemed fazed or to be putting any effort into holding the irate man, and no one was making a move to stop him. The band had stopped playing and the club had gone quiet. All eyes were on the drama that was unfolding.

"Apologize." Table's voice rang out even though he

wasn't yelling. "Apologize to the lady. Now."

The man garbled and choked out an "I'm sorry" before Table flung him to the floor.

"Get your ass out of this bar and don't come back." Table's tone was colder than arctic ice and I could see him vibrate with rage. "If you ever touch another woman like that again and I find out about it, I will hunt you down and make you sorrier."

The man nodded once and crawled to his knees. Table looked at the Dragon Runner holding the waitress and nodded. Then he looked at me and frowned.

He came over to me, and even if I'd wanted to run, I couldn't. He lifted a hand to my cheek and stared deep at me, gentle concern written all over his face. I stared back, getting lost in the depths of his eyes, seeing flecks of green in the brown irises. The world was so gray; the only color in it was him.

"Breathe, Lori." His voice was as soft and low as when he was working with the farm horse or speaking to his baby daughter.

I gasped, not realizing I'd been holding my breath. The gray world disappeared and the noise of the bar returned.

"You okay?" he whispered to me. "Thought I'd lost you there for a minute."

"I'm good," I panted, drawing in as much air as I could, quelling my racing heart and rising stomach.

Anita and Connie came up. Worry was on Anita's face, but Connie was fuming.

"That was Maddie that rat bastard had a hold on. She's

a single mom with three kids. Does some work for me from time to time. Her husband took off and left her for a younger model and now she's subbin' at the school during the day and waitressing here on weekends to make ends meet. She don't need that kind of shit in her life!"

Table glanced at her. "Maddie'll be taken care of. Ain't no man gonna put his hands on a woman and get away with it in this bar. 'Specially when she works for the club."

Club? I must have said it out loud, because Table's attention came back to me.

"Yeah, baby girl. The Dragon Runners MC. Motorcycle club. Asheville chapter. Not as big as the original charter in Bryson City, but still sizable enough."

Club. Not a gang?

"*Chingada,* Lori! You're whiter than a sheet!" Anita's worry caught my attention. "You need to sit down before you fall over!"

"I'm good." The gray fog in my head disappeared altogether and I found myself the center of a very concerned circle. Table was still holding me by my arms, as if keeping me upright. The biggest surprise? I didn't mind.

"Come on, *chica*. Party's over for tonight. You can crash at our place if you want. You don't need to drive all the way back to that farm tonight." Connie made motions to the door.

"I'll take her home," Table stated. "Goin' to the same place, so it's no big deal. She can ride on the back of my bike for that long."

"What about her van?"

"I'll have one of the brothers here drive it back to the farm later. It'll be there in the morning." Table reached out his hand. "Give me your keys, baby girl."

I clutched them to my chest, suddenly feeling suffocated. "No, I'm good. I'll get my van and drive myself. Thanks anyway."

His face showed concern. "Lori, you really don't look too steady. How much have you been drinking tonight?"

I gritted my teeth and pulled sharply away from him, freeing myself from his hold. "I said I'm good. I'm fine. Quit pushing me!"

He raised his hands and stepped back from me. "Okay, fine. Just trying to help."

"If I want your help, I'll ask for it."

His jaw flexed and I knew I'd stepped in it again. "Suit yourself."

"Easy, *chica.* He's not the bad guy." Connie waved a hand in front of my face. "Let's get outta here and into some tequila I have at the house. The band is packing up soon anyway and last call is not far off."

I looked up to see Table rejoining his fellow Runners at the pool tables. He lifted the cue still in his hand, and examined the position of the colored balls. He leaned over, lined up a shot, and stroked the cue stick smoothly, pocketing another ball. He didn't look in my direction again at all. I felt the shame of my acidic response to him and the need to apologize again. Instead, I left with the sisters.

Whatever buzz I'd had going earlier had disappeared with the adrenaline surge. I didn't stay at Connie and

Anita's place but thanked them profusely for a great night out. "Sorry for freaking out so bad. I've never been around a bar fight before and it got to me. I hope your friend Maddie will be okay."

Connie fluffed it off and gave me a big hug. "No problem. The Runners keep a tight ship, just so you know. They don't allow no trouble and Maddie will be just fine. That Runner who had a hold of her when Table was whupping up on that asshole? That's Chevy, and he's been into her a long time. Believe me, she ain't got nothin' to worry about." She drew her eyebrows together and gave me a piercing look. "You, on the other hand, need to settle your ass down. What the hell was that with Table?"

I sighed. "Nothing. Nothing at all. I was just freaked. That's all."

Connie wasn't buying it. "You sure you need to drive back to that farm you're staying at? It's a good thirty minutes from here."

"I'll be fine. I'm sober and I need to be around my own stuff. You know what I mean?"

Anita chimed in. "Stop badgering the woman, Connie. Had a great time tonight, Lori. We'll have to do it again next weekend!"

It had been a nice night up until that asshole decided to pick a fight with a waitress. I lay in my bed, tired as hell but still tossing restlessly, until I heard the growl of Table's motorcycle coming up the driveway. I felt awful about attacking him again when he clearly didn't deserve it. I, more than anyone else in the world, knew there were only so many times forgiveness could be granted before it ran out.

CHAPTER 5

The sound blasting from the speakers was awful. Some local grunge metal band that made more noise than music and had lyrics so depressing, Table was ready to jab the tattoo needle in his ears. The other artists felt the same way, except for the one who'd brought in the recording on his phone.

You can nevurrrrr luv me, so you should die-eeeeee!

"What the fuck is this shit?" Jack Rogers, the owner of the parlor, yelled. He had just walked in carrying four paper sacks with greasy burgers and fries from a local fast food joint.

Bantum looked up from where he was finishing up a small tattoo of a rose on a woman's left breast. She was cringing with every buzz but determined to see it through. That's the way it was with tourists who wandered in and on impulse decided to get inked. Table wondered how many of them regretted it once they got home.

"Ain't it great, bossman? You can hear the angst in his voice speaking to the souls of the people, laying out the true colors of the world in only a few chords!"

Table grunted and went back to the piece he was finishing. This one was an intricate black tribal sleeve, and he was on the third and final session for the complicated design.

"Souls of the people is right! That shit's enough to wake the dead."

No one made a move to change the tunes, though. The agreement was that every hour someone got to pick a station, CD, or whatever music to play and you weren't allowed to argue, just grin and bear it. This worked well until someone got pissed, then all sorts of crap got played. Table had been through nights where the music swung from loud eighties pop to orchestral classic symphonies, from head-banging heavy metal to Broadway show tunes, or from twanging bluegrass to Tibetan singing bowls, of all things. Where the hell Chrissie had found that particular CD treasure was beyond his comprehension. Table suspected she periodically dug to the bottom of the huge flea market CD bargain bins to find most obscure and weird stuff just to mess with the guys in the shop. As the only female tattoo artist in the place, Chrissie made it a point to hold her own against the sea of testosterone she faced on a nightly basis, and did so with her own bold style.

The CD gave one last wail and finished. Chrissie jumped up and started her pick for the night. The strains of opera wafted through the room. Jack let out a giant *GAH!* and disappeared into his office. Chrissie chuckled and sang along with the Italian words.

"Y'all are nuts in here," Ditchdigger said as Table

switched to a bigger tip with more needles. Just one more bit to fill in and the tattoo would be finished.

"Yeah, brother, they are, but they're still good people." Table loaded the needles and started again.

"You goin' to shoot some pool later? You ain't been at the club since that takedown you made. Helluva night, man. Maddie's hooked up with Chevy now and looks like that's gonna be a thing. I wouldn't be surprised if she's an old lady by Christmas. What's the deal with them two Mexican women who were there? You know the name of the short one?"

Table eyed Ditchdigger and dipped more ink. "Name's Connie, and don't go there 'less you think it'll stick."

"Oh, I'll stick it, all right!" Ditchdigger chortled. "I got me a taste for something spicy!"

Table wasn't amused. "I mean it, Ditch. She's a good woman. Has her own business and works hard to keep it. She don't need someone wasting her time. If you're just looking to get your dick wet you'd best keep with the club bunnies."

Ditchdigger laughed again. "Listen to you being all big brother and shit! I'm sure Miss Connie can handle me."

"*All'alba vincerò! Vincerà! Vincerò—*"

The music cut off abruptly and Table looked up in irritation. He wasn't a big fan of opera, but shutting off the CD player midsong was just wrong.

"What the hell, Chrissie?" he asked.

She fluffed her bright blue tinted hair and replied casually over her shoulder, "I just finished my last client and it's midnight-thirty. No one is in the waiting area and the shop's dead, so I'm buggin' out and finding a party somewhere. Laters."

Table sighed and reached for the TV remote. The flat-screen hanging from a corner in the ceiling blinked on as he went back to work.

"The Townsend Foundation annual gala ball has reported a record amount of funds raised this year. Senator Jeffrey Townsend, who recently announced he will be running for another term in office, hosted the ball in place of his son, Jeffrey Junior, the current CEO of Townsend Industries, who has been in Africa for the past year with his wife, Vivian, establishing another humanitarian project school."

The news reporter was blonde and perky and easy to tune out. Table resumed work, and Ditch hissed as the needles dug into his skin once more.

"Fuck, man! That shit stings! If I gotta watch some shit TV while you're stickin' me at least put on some damn sports. I don't give a shit 'bout no fuckin' senator in DC, man!"

Table silently flipped the channel to ESPN where the sports highlights of the week were being shown. His back tightened painfully and he was feeling every one of his thirty-nine years. Forty was just around the corner. He dipped more ink as Ditch guffawed and made comments about whatever game he was watching. The needles buzzed almost soothingly as he colored in the lines he had already drawn. This was not where he had planned to be in his life at this age, but this was where he'd ended up. It could always be worse. His best friend, Blue, had always told him he was too optimistic, always trying to find the brighter side of things, looking for the good in every situation, counting blessings and all that kind of shit. Blue had been dealt a rough hand recently with his ex-wife and a bitter custody battle over the kids, and got irritated every time he talked to Table about it. He was constantly telling Blue life would get better, and then Blue complained about Table's sunny outlook.

He recalled their last face-to-face conversation before he left Bryson City.

"You're too fucking patient with that shit. You've got a great thing going here with the business, you're solid in the club, rising in the ranks, 'n' gotta good chance to date a good woman for a change. You gotta future here, man, and you're gonna give it up and go raise a kid you don't know is yours."

Table had eyed him speculatively. "You're one to talk, brother. Angel is mine, no doubt about it, and I'm gonna need some help. Your mama would jump in with both feet but she's got her own grandkids to think about. Besides, what's the alternative? Put my kid in foster care so I can keep partyin' and playin'? Fuck that. I can either wallow in it or do something about it. You know me, brother. I ain't about to wallow."

"You almost done?" Ditch's whining broke into his thoughts

"Almost. Now hold still, fucker."

The TV droned on and Ditch squirmed until Table announced the tattoo was finished. Ditch stayed long enough to get his arm gelled and wrapped, and gave only half an ear to the aftercare instructions Table was reciting.

"Yeah, brother, I know, I know. I gotta bolt. See ya!"

Table had a feeling Ditch was looking for the party Chrissie had gone to, probably to score a night with the blue-haired and pierced girl. Oh, to be young again. Nope, he'd had enough of the party-every-night-till-dawn life. Now it was fatherhood, which was almost a bigger challenge than running the Tail of the Dragon, a road famous for its quick and sharp turns. He was living in one big curve with plenty more up ahead.

Table cleaned his equipment carefully and eyed the dirty stuff left behind by the other two artists who'd jetted just as soon as they could from the store. It would never have been allowed at the shop he'd run in Bryson City, but here he was not the owner or manager. It was just a part-time gig to earn some money while he figured out his next move.

Table mounted his bike and left the downtown shop for home. The nights were getting cooler, but as long as he could ride, he would. Freedom on his bike was something he relished and from time to time he thought about when he would get Angel her first bike and teach her the joys of riding.

He geared down and guided the bike into the garage, careful not to make any more noise than he had to. More than once he'd been up with Angel during the night and seen Lori's light come on. The woman was prickly and exasperating, and had pissed him off more than once, but there was still a fragility about her he couldn't quite pinpoint.

He was on his way to the main house when he saw her leave the upper room and carefully make her way down the narrow steps and head toward the creek. He wanted nothing more than to go in the house, check on his beautiful sleeping girl, and crash face-first into his own bed. Instead, he found himself following the petite woman.

* * *

I shot up in the bed, gasping as if there were hands tightening on my throat. I clawed at the comforter, trying to escape it, and ended up falling to the hard floor with a loud thump. My hip and elbow throbbed from the impact, but the sudden pain helped pull me out of the nightmare. I was in my little remote room, in a little remote town, in a little remote part of the state. I was okay. I was safe.

I got up and went to the small fridge where I kept a water bottle and gulped the cold liquid, wetting my dry mouth and cooling my sweating body. Someday, I hoped these damn nightmares would stop. Maybe once it was over, I could finally be free.

Earlier today I had texted a New Jersey number, asking for an update. It took a lot of time to text from my phone as I had to scroll through the letters one at a time on the outdated keypad, but I eventually did get the message out. When it was answered, I was disappointed to hear there was another delay—but to not worry about it.

Not worry? This was the third delay and had the potential

to keep me in this limbo state for weeks, maybe months. I was frustrated and mad about it, and wanted to throw something against a wall just to watch it break. I ended up snapping my cell phone in half and tossing it in a dumpster. It was time for me to get a new burner anyway. Maybe I'd watched too many spy movies and thought it was easy to track someone through cell phone towers, but I still didn't want to take any chances.

Sleep was not coming back to me anytime soon. I threw on some sweatpants and an oversized hoodie, as nights in the mountains could get cold. I stepped outside, listening to the burble of the river as it flowed over rocks and the light chittering of crickets and other bugs. The moon was full in the dark sky as I made my way down to part of the bank that overlooked the wide creek, letting the peaceful sounds rush over my raw nerves. Nothing had been going right lately. The winter garden wasn't producing like the sisters wanted and I felt like I was to blame for it. One of the ATV's tires shredded while I was riding it back to the house one afternoon. A tire on one vehicle shouldn't have been a big deal, but the same ATV had also broken a belt recently. Table had put it down to regular maintenance needing to be done, but the parade of problems still had me tied in knots.

"You all right?"

I screamed and jumped three feet in the air at the unexpected voice. I nearly slipped and fell down the embankment, which wouldn't have been life threatening but would not have made my night any more fun.

"Sorry, Lori. Didn't mean to scare you none. I saw you

leave your place when I was comin' down the driveway and just wanted to check on you." Table appeared, dressed in worn jeans, black leather jacket that I knew had his club insignia on the back, and a black knit hat on his head. "Damn, baby girl! You're white as a ghost. What's wrong?"

"Nothing," I answered quickly. "Just couldn't sleep and decided to come outside for a bit."

Table grunted an acknowledgment but didn't go back to the big house. We hadn't said much to each other since the night of the club fight. These were the first words we'd spoken besides the *have-a-nice-day* moment when we shared breakfast with Martha and Carol in the mornings and farm talk. That was the sum total of our recent contact. Now, he came up to stand next to me and I could feel his presence like something solid. He reached down and picked up a handful of sharp gravel. "Are you sure 'bout that 'nothin',' Lori?"

I took in a sharp breath. "What do you mean?"

He fingered a pebble, tossing it lightly into the water. I heard a faint plop.

"I just think there may be somethin' to your nothin'. I'm not a college man, but I'm not stupid and I got eyes in my head."

He tossed in another pebble, this time skimming it across the moonlit surface.

"The first morning I met you when you came up to the house with your hands all chewed up by the chicken, you looked lost."

He skimmed another pebble. I wrapped my arms

defensively around myself as I braced for more words.

"I know you don't sleep good at night 'cause I see the lights on when I get home. You're jumpy as shit most of the time. You ain't got any real property other than your van and I'm bettin' there's not a long paper trail on it. I'm also bettin' your name ain't Lori Matthews either 'cause the information you wrote down on the contract is bogus. Martha thinks you're a free spirit or some sort of bullshit hippie pilgrim. Carol thinks you're escaping from a cult and is determined to 'save' you. I'm not sure what to think, but I've watched you bite at me twice so far, fightin' back against a threat that don't exist and then runnin' away like a scared, whipped, stray dog. Right now I'm looking at you, huggin' yourself like you're trying not to fall apart. I can't help but feel you got somethin' more than nothin'. Makes me wonder what kind of demons you got chasing you."

I was lost for a moment at his bluntness, and then I burred up. "No, I'm not a free spirit hippie cultist and any demons I have I can handle myself. I'm not a criminal on the run either."

He grunted and skimmed again, the pebble bouncing three times before sinking into the water.

"I told you I got eyes in my head, right? I've seen how hard you work and how tight you hold your shit together. I've watched you with my daughter and how you take care of them like they were your own people. I don't think someone with criminal intent would've stuck around this long, takin' care of two old ladies plus watchin' out for a baby."

He threw the last of the rocks into the creek, no skimming this time. He turned and faced me direct.

This was it. He was going to tell me to pack up and get out, and I was fully prepared for that. What I wasn't prepared for were his next words.

"I ain't exactly lily-white when it comes to followin' the law. The Dragon Runners are a legit club but weren't always, and there are times when us and the law still clash a bit. Brick, our president, says there's sometimes a difference between what's right by law and what justice is, and I happen to agree with him. You can't judge everything by one yard stick. I think maybe you're runnin' from somethin'. I don't know what it is, but I ain't seen anything that tells me you're a bad person. The club protects its own and while you're living under my roof, that protection extends to you even if you don't want it. It would be nice to get a heads-up if you can do that for me."

A feeling rustled in my gut, both unnerving and relieving. "No demons, Table," I managed to say firmly, but I couldn't meet his eyes as I spoke. "*If* I'm running from something, I promise there's no blowback on you or Martha and Carol. I'd leave tomorrow if I thought that would happen."

His soft sentence almost undid me. "I'm a pretty good demon-slayer, baby girl."

I felt tears hit my eyes and I had to retreat before I burst. "I'm heading to bed. Have a nice night."

I could sense his eyes on me as I turned and walked back to my room. I didn't turn around even though I wanted to. I was afraid if I did, I would start running back to him.

CHAPTER 6

I tucked my hands in my jacket and swore again that I would buy gloves the next time I forced myself to go shopping. The sun was out and there was no wind, but it was still around sixty degrees and cold. I supposed that was normal in the mountains in mid-November.

I was helping Martha with their vendor booth at the North Asheville Tailgate market. Carol usually did this chore, but today she was under the weather and I was asked if I could fill in. This was the last Saturday the market would be open and the crowd was enormous. Hundreds of people were out and about, probably in preparation for the upcoming Thanksgiving holiday. The canopy-covered stalls were arranged in long lines along a paved parking lot at the University of North Carolina at Asheville campus. Homegrown vegetables, breads and other sweets, cheeses, handwoven rugs, plants, crafted jewelry... the variety of stuff for sale was mind-boggling. There was even a duo of violin and mandolin at one booth playing Christmas tunes for tips.

Christmas! I couldn't believe I'd been in this place long enough to get to the holidays.

Martha and I had been there since 6:00 a.m., setting up the double canopy and putting out the last of the vegetables for sale. Potatoes, sweet pumpkins for baking, acorn squash, and something called a cushaw were piled on the white plastic-covered tables. I'd never heard of or seen the green-striped oblong vegetable before, but Martha explained it was another kind of squash good for baking pies.

"Carol's gonna make up two cushaw pies for Thanksgivin' dinner next week. Tastes a little like sweet tater pie."

Since I'd never tasted a sweet potato either, I didn't have a clue what that meant.

It was getting close to the noon closing time when Table showed up carrying a bright-eyed Angel bundled up in a thick one-piece outfit that made her look like a yellow duck. A pacifier was attached to the zipper with an orange ribbon and made to look like a bill. Martha scowled at him. "Whatcha done with that stroller I bought'cha?"

Table grinned and jostled Angel, who was looking around. "Now how tough do you think I'm gonna look wearing my club colors and pushing around a baby stroller? You're messin' with my street cred!"

Martha scoffed at him. "Street cred, my ass! You jus' keep on thinking you look real rough 'n' tough while you got a duckling over your shoulder." She went back to puttering around and rearranging the remaining produce. I stifled a laugh and he grinned even larger.

Maybe this was the reason I stuck around. The easy family atmosphere and the support I'd seen and experienced from these people was far from what I was used to. I was finding myself craving the fellowship more and more. I'd even ventured to church with Carol a few times and found out my presence lowered the average age there by at least a decade. Table was a big part of it. The truce between us was mainly due to his easy manner and his show of character. He worked hard and took care of his family and no one could dispute his dedication to his little girl. His real name was James and occasionally Jimmy-boy if Martha was mad at him. He seemed to take life in stride and spent more time with his daughter than any other father I knew. I'd still not seen any sign of Angel's mother, and although I was curious, I never asked. Table talked a lot, joked a lot, put up with Martha's cantankerous mood and Carol's constant preaching and praying. The only time I'd ever seen him lose his temper was with me the evening we confronted each other in the garden. The other time I snapped at him at the bar, he just left me alone. Even then he wasn't half as bad as other people I know.

"Hey, Nanny M! Whassup?"

I spotted a tall, dark-haired man heading toward us through the crowd of people. He was wearing a jacket and I recognized the insignia of Table's motorcycle club. He must be a member, or as Table would say, a brother. To my surprise, he had an arm slung around a familiar figure. Connie had been talking about a biker who had been badgering her for a date. She finally gave in and went out with him. Apparently, it went well and this was him.

"Lori! *Chica*! How's it going?" Her face had a big happy smile plastered across it and she had an arm around the man's solid waist.

The man looked perplexed for a moment. "You two know each other?"

Connie rolled her eyes. "*Si, cariño,* we work together. She's the skinny white girl I told you about. *Chingada!*"

"Get your ass outta the way, Ditchdigger! You're blockin' my customers!" Martha had finished puttering and was ordering the big scary biker around like she would a child.

Ditchdigger laughed and took his arm off Connie to wrap it around the old woman in a big bear hug. "I love you too, Nanny."

"Dang it, you're like a hair in a biscuit. Always hangin' round. Turn me loose!" The old woman groused at the giant, but it was obvious she enjoyed the attention.

"We doing Thanksgiving dinner at your place, right?" The question was directed at Table, but Martha answered.

"If the weather's warm enough, gonna be outside. Got maybe forty or so people comin' 'n' that's too many t' fit in the big house. If it's too cold or we get any weather, gonna be at the church. Carol's got a key t' the big dinner room. Either way you need t' come early and help set up."

"Church?" Ditchdigger's eyes got comically big. "I don't know 'bout that. I could get struck by lightning if I walk through the door!"

"Preacher don't have no job 'less he's got sinners t' save.

Just don't say nothin' to Carol. She's longer winded than him."

I was still trying to get my head around the words "Thanksgiving dinner" and "forty people or so." Table noticed my slack look. "There a lot of aunts, uncles, cousins, and kids that come around on Thanksgiving. It ends up being a gigantic potluck with all-day eating. This year, I invited some of my club brothers from the Asheville chapter. Some of them don't have another place to go and this is a time when it's all about family and connections."

"I'm making *enchiladas* with homemade *mole* sauce," Connie trilled, back under Ditchdigger's arm again. "You got a special somethin', *chica*?"

I stuttered. "I'm—uh—not invited."

Table looked at me funny and shifted duckie Angel to his other shoulder. "Why would you think that?"

"Um—I'm not really family."

Table's face was unreadable, but his answer was clear. "Yes, you are."

The tension of the moment was gone when Ditchdigger declared, "I'm bringing the booze!"

"You ain't bringing no booze t' the church! You'll give Carol a heart attack and I'll hafta deal with her preachin' hellfire and damnation till the New Year!" Martha shook a finger at the behemoth. Table roared with laughter as I watched. He lifted a finger to wipe his eye.

"Lord, I needed that. Good thing the harvesting is done. The tractor threw a rod this morning up in the field. Oil was run out dry, which doesn't make a lot of sense 'cause I checked it last week. Ditch is gonna help me tow it back, but I'll still need to get a new part and patch the shaft."

"Ain't had no problem with that tractor in thirty years. Might be there's a part in the storage shed." Martha started boxing up the remaining few vegetables. "You best be gettin' to it, if you 's expectin' to get that done tonight."

I went to help Martha with the loading and Table stopped me by placing Angel in my arms.

"Ditch and I will take care of the loading, Nanny. You ladies can discuss where we're goin' for lunch. My treat."

"Woo hoo! Dude done messed it up! Hey, baby, google up one a them fancy-ass restaurants that has more than one fork next to the plate," Ditchdigger directed Connie with a big goofy grin as he heaved a box into the bed of Martha's truck.

She rolled her eyes as she huffed and pulled out her phone. I ignored both of them as I held the small, squirming bundle. Angel regarded me with her daddy's brown eyes and a wrinkled-up forehead. Even though I'd held her many times already, she didn't quite know what to make of me, but she wasn't crying or fussing.

"Hello, precious," I whispered. "It's Lori. Lo-wree."

Angel's face relaxed into a toothless smile and she made a cooing noise in greeting.

"I like your duckie outfit. It's very pretty. Pretty outfit for a pretty girl." I found myself swaying back and forth in a rocking motion. Connie was scrolling through her phone, and Martha was directing the two men. The rest of the market noise died away as I chattered away at the baby.

"You're a daddy's girl for sure. Your daddy is a really nice man."

Angel waved her cloth-covered hand and tried to grab my lip. She let out a "ba-ba-ba" in agreement and blew a wet raspberry. I couldn't help myself. I was totally in love with the adorable little bundle. She was surrounded by people who loved her and saw to her every need, treating her like the princess she was. She would never be hungry. She would never suffer pain. She would never be forced to do something she didn't want to do. She would live her life knowing she had an entire village of people supporting her no matter what. I envied that a bit.

I felt a tingle at the back of my neck and looked up into Table's soft gaze. His eyes touched me and I was drawn into them. Something was changing in me. No, not changing. I was rediscovering a part of myself I'd thought I'd lost. I had already noted my admiration of this man as a father and as a grandson. I had seen his abilities once as a lover. He had laid out his concerns that night at the creek and instead of giving me the boot, he had given me his vow of protection. Now I found myself looking at him as a man worthy of my trust. I found it exhilarating and a bit terrifying; this was a new feeling and I didn't know what to do with it.

Table seemed to sense something was happening with me. Something monumental that he didn't quite understand, but was a good way to be. His solemn face transformed as he nodded and winked at me.

"Truck's loaded 'n' ready. I ain't doing no fancy lunch. I need to get on back to th' house an' check on Carol."

Martha's dry voice pierced the air. She seemed blithely unaware of the magnitude of what had just happened. Then again, if a sudden tornado had just whipped through the market, leaving behind broken stalls, piles of debris, and injuries, I'd bet every last hoarded dollar I had that the first thing out of her mouth would be, "Whelp, we got work to do. Let's get to cleanin'."

"All right, Nanny. Can you take Angel home for me? She's needs a change and a nap. I'll unload the truck when I get there in about an hour or so."

Martha grunted, which he took to mean "yes," and he loaded the sleepy child into the car seat that was kept in the back of the extended cab. Table had another one in the back of his truck's cab as well.

Home. I was starting to use that word more and more about these people. I had mixed feelings about that. I wanted a home. I wanted to have a place where I belonged and that had space just for me. There was that possibility here, but in giving me that place, there was a risk they didn't know about. If they did, would I still have a place?

My brain spun in circles as we drove into downtown Asheville to go to a local brewery restaurant, Wicked Weed. We had to park in a crowded parking garage, as finding a street space for Table's big truck was an issue. Ditch and Connie had ridden Ditch's motorcycle and didn't have any trouble finding a spot close by.

We sat on the patio despite the chilly air. I didn't particularly like cold weather, but it didn't seem to faze the other three. There were several heaters on the patio, which helped. Music was played quietly over outdoor speakers. We took more time ordering beers than we did burgers, as the selection of different beers was huge.

Table handed me a menu. "Get whatever you want, baby girl. If you can't make up your mind, try a flight. I'm only having one seeing as I'm driving and I gotta work later. You got big plans tonight?"

I wondered if this was a trick question. "An exciting night of housework for Martha and Carol, followed by laundry and maybe a date with a book."

"Hmm, you've got it as good as I do. Next free night, we'll go for a ride if it ain't too cold for you." He tapped a few beer selections on the menu to the hovering waitress.

A flutter clenched my stomach, but I didn't freeze up at the thought of riding on the back of a motorcycle. The beers and food came quickly, and the conversation turned to other subjects. Ditch and Table talked about bike rides, rallies, the River's Edge bar, some place called the Lair, and other members of the club.

"I heard Mute got hisself an old lady. Nurse down at the hospital," Ditch said, draping an arm around Connie's shoulders. It seemed if he was anywhere in proximity to her, he was going to be touching her. Connie didn't seem to mind.

"Yeah, he did. Fucker deserves some happiness in his life." Table took a sip of the beer he had ordered.

"No doubt about that. Heard tell Stud's down as well. Word is he's got a bun in his lady's oven. Never thought I'd see that brother settle down. Too wild for women, the skankier the better, but as I've been told, he's completely and totally done for." Ditch took a healthy swallow of a darker brew.

Table's face changed a bit. "Yeah, Stud's a lucky man."

I wondered what that meant, but Ditch kept going.

"Word is Blue's having trouble again with his ex. Finally got rid of her. A real bitch, that one! Shoulda scraped her ass off long ago. Still fightin' with her sorry ass from what I hear." Ditch sniffed and poked a french fry into a pond of ketchup on his plate.

"Give him a little credit, man. He's got two kids by her and was tryin' to make it work for their sake. Man's got more at stake than his pride when it comes to his children." Table swallowed a big bite of burger. "I know better 'n most about trying to make it work."

Ditch looked both ridiculous and contrite with the red sauce smeared across his face. "Sorry, brother. I forgot you got troubles like that."

"I *had* trouble like that. Tamara is long gone. I have no idea where she went or who she's with now."

I couldn't help myself. "Did you love her?" My voice was small but my words seemed to jar him. He looked at me, those beautiful brown eyes deep and honest.

"I thought I did. Love dies with betrayal."

There wasn't much I could say after a comment like that that. We finished up, said our goodbyes, and left. Table led me back to the truck and opened the door for me to climb in. The silence in the cab was uncomfortable and he turned on the radio for a little noise. Country music filled the air, but I only listened with half an ear. Table sensed the change in me and wisely stayed silent the rest of the drive.

Back at the farm, Table and I quickly unloaded the truck and put away the heavier stuff that Martha couldn't manage. I went to my room and he went into the big house to spend more time with his daughter before he had to go to work. After he left, I spent an exciting Saturday night mopping a kitchen floor and scrubbing toilets. The ladies were by no means sloppy in their living habits, but dirt still happened and needed to be cleaned.

Angel was a gem as always, cooing and rolling around on a giant blanket on the wood floor in the TV room. Carol was eased back in her recliner, covered with several of her knitted afghans and watching some entertainment gossip show on the giant flat-screen TV. Martha was puttering around the house, trying to find something to do with her hands.

"Opening night at the Kennedy Center with the National Symphony Orchestra featuring rising opera star Genevieve Blandford. Her voice is incredible!"

"Yes, indeed it is! What do you think it's like to be that young and talented?"

"I don't know, but check out her husband, Victor Blandford, in the front row balcony."

"Did you notice Senator Townsend is attending? He's one of the big supporters of the arts through his daughter-in-law's foundation."

"I'm surprised to see him here with all the hullaballoo on the hill. The senator is making other news now with

the scandalous investigation of his finances. The search is on for his son and daughter-in-law, Jeffrey Jr. and Vivian Townsend, since their family foundation is part of the investigation. The authorities are saying they went to South Africa on a humanitarian and philanthropic mission for the Townsend Foundation and haven't been back in the country for over a year."

"Rumors are abounding now, Phil, since a picture has surfaced on social media of Jeffrey Townsend piloting a speedboat around Rio De Janeiro. Sources say that he has been seen in the company of several fashion models, but no one has seen Mrs. Townsend with him yet."

"Hmm—that bears for speculation, eh?"

"It sure does, Phil, but tonight we're here for some wonderful music. The curtain to the season is about to rise, folks!"

My palms started sweating around the mop handle I was pushing across the linoleum kitchen floor. I could see the TV screen from my position, and though the picture was now of the two hosts, the photo they'd shown was burned into my brain. A handsome man, his tanned chest shiny with sweat or oil, in an expensive-looking boat with the wind blowing his dark blond hair back. He was smiling a brilliant white smile and wearing dark sunglasses. Next to him was a thin brunette woman in tiny strips of cloth some may call a bikini. She was also wearing dark sunglasses. Two perfect people. The camera's date stamp stated the picture was taken only a week ago. My heart pounded and the blood roared in my ears.

The spell broke when the image changed again to the home shopping network. Two women were extolling the virtues of an immersion stick blender and I blinked at the sudden change.

"What the hell happened to the TV?" Martha yelled from a back room.

"It's time for the kitchen stuff for sale." Carol shifted her mound of yarn blankets to the side. "Imma gettin' some tea."

"The floor's wet. I'll get it for you."

I shuffled on the wet linoleum and nuked a cup of water in the microwave.

A few minutes later, Carol took the steaming mug from my hand. "Oh, that's wonderful, dear! We're so glad to have you here." The old woman took a cautious sip of the hot brew and settled back in her chair. Angel cooed, waving her hands, and heaved herself over onto her stomach. She was getting more and more active. It wouldn't be long before she figured out how to crawl. I put the news piece to rest as I eyed a few of the lower shelves and the knickknacks that would have to be moved and stored someplace else.

I helped Martha bathe Angel and get her ready for bed. The soft baby scent wafted to my nostrils as she curled up in the pretty white crib, her round diapered bottom stuck straight in the air, secure in the love this household had for her.

Later, in my bed, I remembered the photo of the playboy and his model. My head churned and I got up to check the lock on the door. I lay awake for the rest of the night, staring at the ceiling until the pale fingers of dawn crept through the windows. *Someday.* My mind cycled the word over and over again. *Someday.*

CHAPTER 7

I found out how fickle North Carolina weather could be at Thanksgiving. One week, it was cold, wet, and snowy, and the next week the temperatures had risen up to over seventy degrees and the skies were as bright and sunny as a summer day. I'd spent the last few days on double duty, cleaning houses for the upcoming holiday with Connie and helping Martha and Carol prepare their big holiday meal. Instead of using the ovens in the kitchen, Martha had lined up a bunch of huge mismatched Crock-Pots to roast a variety of different meats. Wild turkey, deer, beef tips, and a couple of gigantic hams were all bubbling away on the counters in the kitchen. Outside, Table and some of his cousins were setting up folding tables and chairs that had been unearthed from the storage building. Some of the people there were from the Dragon Runners, wearing their club insignias. Table had laughed when I called them vests and informed me they were called "cuts." Martha huffed and simply stated, "They's all family here."

Everyone brought a dish of some sort. It seemed like the women and a few of the men were in competition to see who could make the best of the best of homemade foods. Vegetables, casseroles, salads, breads, and a small mountain of desserts were spread out over the plastic-covered tables. I was glad that the weather had changed, as I was sure this many people and this much food would never have fit inside the house and maybe not the small church either. As it was, Carol said the blessing over the food as it was being set out and people served themselves buffet style.

Table looked like he was having the time of his life, walking around and greeting people with Angel, dressed up in a turkey onesie, in his arms. He wore his own Dragon Runners cut over a black Henley, worn blue jeans that molded his behind into something special, and his heavy black boots. His bald head was bare except for the dark sunglasses he had perched on top. Every inch of him declared him to be a baddass biker, and I was hyperaware of him all day.

"Martha tells me you've been a big help to them this fall." An older man came up to me as I was moving casserole dishes around on the table to make room for more. I couldn't remember his name, but I knew he was one of Carol's sons.

"They've been good to me and I've learned a lot about maintaining a garden." I heard Table's laugh and glanced up to see him standing next to a blonde woman—the one I'd seen him with my first night at the farm. A thread of jealousy ran through me as I watched the easy way Table acted around her. Charlotte was her name, as I recalled, and the sudden spurt of possessiveness caught me off guard. Then I saw another Dragon Runner come up to them, put his arm around the woman, and tilt her head back for a long kiss. Her hand came up and caressed the man's cheek and I spotted the flash of a diamond on her finger. Table didn't flinch or get angry. He laughed even louder and seemed happy to be shaking the man's hand in a congratulatory movement. Charlotte smiled and nodded, her eyes on the man who was obviously her fiancé.

"I'd say you've been good to all of us. Them two women are stubborn as hell about this farm and keeping it going. It's too much for them sometimes, but James is a good one. Makes some trouble sometimes with his biker friends, but still a good man to have at your back."

My ears burned a little. "Trouble?" I asked, trying to sound casual and only semi-interested in the answer.

The man shrugged and flopped his hand dismissively. "Nothin' big. Just rowdy sometimes. Got into some fights 'n stuff like that. He was a wild one back in high school, but the military straightened him out right quick. Did a couple of tours in Afghanistan before coming home. Still had some trouble, but managed to keep his nose clean. Pretty amazing he's turned out to be the way his is even after his upbringing."

I wanted to ask more, but a loud roar sounded, grabbing everyone's attention. Two large motorcycles carrying two people each came rolling down the gravel driveway. I saw Table out of the corner of my eye throw back his head and let out a howl. Angel looked startled at the noise, but instead of crying she raised up a tiny hand and popped her daddy in the mouth. I stifled a giggle. Table looked up, walked over, and pushed Angel into my arms before dragging us both to meet the newcomers.

A woman dismounted from one bike and removed her helmet, shaking out her long curly ginger hair. "See? I told you it was this driveway! But noooo! The big studly man can't take directions from a woman! Took two wrong turns and three double backs before you finally listened."

"Ease up, Cactus." The man laughed as he dismounted and removed his own helmet. He was one of the most handsome men I'd ever seen, with gorgeous long blond hair and Chris Hemsworth blue eyes. "You know men don't ask for directions. I told you we'd find it eventually. You feeling okay?"

"No, I gotta pee again and needed it done twenty minutes ago, ya stubborn feck."

"Love you, Eva."

The woman stopped her tirade and her face became tender. "Love you too, *mo rún*. Now where's the bathroom?"

"Straight up in the house, darlin'," Table directed as he approached the quartet. The ginger-haired woman hugged him briefly before making a beeline to the white building. "Stud! Glad you made it, brother! Great to see you." He extended his hand to the Viking god and they pulled in for a man hug accompanied by several back slaps. "I heard Eva's pregnant. What's she doing on the back of your bike?"

Stud shook his head and laughed. "It was either that or she was gonna ride her own. By all means, brother, if you think you can stop her, have at it. Doctor said it was safe for her to ride since she's used to so much physical labor, and she's taken that seriously. Short of tying her to the bed, I can't get her to slow down much."

Table grimaced. "Better you than me, brother. I think she made the right choice when you finally pulled your thumb out."

"Asshole!" Stud said, smiling as if it were a term of affection, and lightly punched Table's shoulder. "Had to rub it in, didn't you?"

Table turned to the other couple. I shivered at the dark look of the ginormous man dismounting from the second, heavier motorcycle and taking off his own helmet. His long black hair was held back in a ponytail and his glowering countenance could freeze someone to the spot. His menacing air was only broken by the petite brunette who slipped under his huge arm and curled into his side, completely comfortable and sure of her welcome.

"Mute! Kat! Great to see you both!" Table approached the scary giant. "I see you gave up the brain buckets and finally got some full face shields."

They repeated the man hug and back slaps. Mute didn't say anything, but Kat thanked Table for the invitation and said that she had some of Betsey's barbeque in the saddlebags for him.

"It's been in the freezer since the Halloween picnic, and probably thawed on the way here, but I'm sure it's still good," Kat stated.

Table acted like she just handed him a bar of gold.

"Oh, Katwoman! If you ever decide to trade up and leave this brute all you have to do is bring me some of Betsey's barbeque and I'll take you on."

Kat laughed lightly at the joke while Mute all but growled.

Table shook it off. "I'm messin' with you, brother. Come meet my best girls." He gestured to me to come closer and my heart fluttered for a moment. He took the baby from my arms to present her to his friends. "This is my little girl. My little Angel," he said with pride. "This is Lori. She's been helping out around here for a while now."

"Nice to meet you, Lori." Kat extended her hand for me to take. Mute didn't say anything, but gave me a sharp nod. From what I gathered about his name and his demeanor, he couldn't talk. Someday, I might know that story.

"Glad to meet anyone who can put up with this bunch! I'm Eva." The ginger-haired woman had returned. I couldn't tell that she was pregnant, but I could tell that she was a strong woman. Not only in attitude, but physically. I was afraid if I tried to shake her hand she would break it just by being friendly.

I noticed all of them had cuts with the same Dragon Runner symbol as Table's, with the exception that the women had "property of" patches sewn above the names of their men. I didn't like it. The concept of a woman being the property of a man was appalling to me, but as I watched the interaction between Eva and Stud, it was hard to recognize her as being property. She stood toe to toe with him throughout the day, and he seemed to love every minute of it. I watched the silent Mute take care of his Kat with a tenderness that belied his don't-fuck-with-me appearance. These were truly devoted people. Table told me in passing that these were two of his closest club brothers from his home chapter in Bryson City. I could hear the longing in his voice as he spoke of the people there. Betsey and Brick, Taz and Tambre, Cutter and Molly; all of those names passed over his lips with respect and I knew he missed this part of his life fiercely.

As the day went on into night, the temperature started dropping and the crowd of people dispersed to their own homes. Table's friends helped to clear and put up the tables, and the women helped put the few leftovers away. They left to go back to a place called the Lair, which was about an hour away, and soon the only adults left on the farm were me, Table, Carol, and Martha. Angel had been up for all that time, not wanting to miss anything, and was getting fussy. Instead of getting frustrated with the whiny baby, Table shushed and crooned at the girl, letting her curl up on his shoulder as he rocked her back and forth on the porch swing. I sat and watched them, a glass of sweet tea in my hand.

He looked at me as the little girl fought to stay awake. "No use trying to put her down until she's ready to go." Cuddled to her daddy's warm body, it didn't take long for the tiny girl to give up and fall asleep. Table lifted her and took her in the house to put her in her crib for the night. Martha and Carol were already inside watching TV and dozing in their respective recliners. I stayed on the porch, sipping my tea and listening to the night sounds. It had been a good day. Table's family was wonderful and the comradery between him and his club brothers was something even tighter than the blood ties he had with his cousins. I found myself envious of that. Envious of the surety Eva showed about Stud's love for her. There was no doubt she was his world. The connection between Kat and Mute was so tangible, you could almost touch it. God, I wanted that in my life!

I shivered as a sudden cold hit me and I lost some of my enthusiasm for being outside. I put the tea glass down on the wicker table next to the chair I was sitting in and hugged my arms around myself. My skin prickled and I felt uneasy. I didn't know why, but something was bugging me. I felt like I was being watched.

I jumped as Table suddenly appeared.

"Damn, baby girl. Didn't mean to scare you. Angel is down for the night and I didn't want to leave you on your own out here. If you're tired, I'll walk you back to your room, or if you want to keep more company, you can always bunk in the big house tonight."

I breathed a little easier in his presence. "No, I'm good. You don't have to walk me to my room. It's not like it's miles away."

Table grinned. "'S no problem, Lori. It won't take long and besides, if I don't walk you, Martha will snatch me bald." He got a comical look on his face and ran a hand over his smooth scalp. "Uh-oh! Too late!"

I couldn't help it. I burst into laughter. It was good to really let go and enjoy the feeling of opening up.

Table's smile got bigger. "Good to see you do that, baby girl. You got a nice laugh and should let it out more often. I got an idea for you. Angel's down for the night 'n' the odd couple are snorin' in their chairs. How 'bout a bike ride? It's a bit chilly but I think you can handle it. What do you say?"

A bike ride? This time of night? Maybe it was the feeling of being a part of such a big family. Maybe it was meeting Table's club brothers and seeing their obvious respect for him. Maybe it was just good old-fashioned hormones. For whatever reason, I found myself wrapped in Martha's heavy winter hunting jacket and straddling the back of Table's motorcycle with a red helmet strapped to my head.

We took off, and I mean took off!

The wind was icy and still pierced through the jacket but I didn't mind. I figured out how to lean slightly into the curves, feeling the pull of inertia as the bike twisted through the winding mountain road Table had chosen. The look of the bushes and trees whipping by in the wide illumination of the bike's headlight was a bit eerie, but where the forest broke there were glimpses of a clear, dark sky dotted with brilliant stars, calming in their stillness. I could barely grip Table's waist with my bare hands. He somehow knew it and reached up to pull me further into him, tucking my freezing hands into the pockets of his leather jacket. I felt his body flexing as he changed gears, braked to slow down, or gunned to speed up. I don't know where Table was heading, but he was in total control and I trusted him.

Shit. I trusted him!

The ride was probably less than ten minutes long and

soon we were pulling back into the farm driveway. Table cut off the rumbling engine and then took my hands out of his pockets to examine them.

"Damn, baby girl. You need some gloves. Real ones, not them stretchy dollar store kind either."

He rubbed my fingers between his and I grew warm from his touch.

We walked slowly through the dark. Table stopped at the narrow steps that led to my room. I turned to thank him for everything and froze. He was standing close, his eyes looking into mine. I was alone in the dark with a man. A man I was aware of and tingling from it. I looked at his generous lips framed by his fantastic beard and had the urge to touch them, just to see if they were as soft as they looked. Forget my fingers. I wanted to put my lips to his. I also wanted to run like hell.

He made the decision for me when he leaned in and kissed my forehead. "'Night, Lori. Sleep well." His voice was rough and low as he gave me a little push toward the stairs. I could still feel the place where his lips had pressed to my skin as I moved up the steep steps. I looked back to see he was still at the bottom, waiting for me to enter my room. I nodded at him; afraid that if I spoke, I'd shatter. He didn't move or stop looking at me until I closed and locked the door. Only then did I hear him walk away.

Sleep didn't come easy. I tossed and turned, incapable of finding a comfortable position and failing to turn off my brain. When I did finally drift off, the nightmares came with such viciousness, I woke up retching, tears clogging my throat. I staggered over to the sink, half-drunk with fatigue, and didn't bother trying to get my water bottle. I just stuck my head under the faucet and gulped at the cold liquid as it filled my mouth. This had to end soon before I went stark, raving mad. I ran my fingers through my shaggy tangled mop of growing hair and recalled the bike ride. The feeling of trust.

I wanted to get back on that motorcycle and never get off.

CHAPTER 8

Table blew one last raspberry on Angel's stomach. The baby went into peals of laughter and slapped her tiny hands around his head. Black Friday was a big deal for retailers and not so much for tattoo artists, but he still had to go open the shop. Whatever had possessed him to agree to a first shift during one of the busiest and heaviest traffic times of the year, he didn't know. But he had agreed and needed to keep his word.

Last night was rough. The day had been great, with good food, good friends, and good family. He hadn't expected the twinge of homesickness for his life in Bryson City to hit him so hard. Seeing the brothers he had prospected alongside and ultimately joined with was tough, and Eva being with Stud was bittersweet on its own. At one time he'd thought he had feelings for Eva, but seeing her and Stud told him she was with the right man.

Lori's presence was adding another complication. One minute she hated and was scared of him, and the next minute she was looking at him like she wanted to devour him whole. Table knew already that something had happened to her. Any fool should be able to tell that someone had done a number on her, but to what extent was still a mystery. Table wished he could find the son of a bitch in a dark alley and take care of the demons that haunted her. Last night, after having her on the back of his bike and as he walked her back to her room, he'd grown hard at the idea of touching her, and it seemed she was becoming more open to the idea every day. Last night, he'd almost given in to the desire to kiss her, and unless he'd gotten his signals badly crossed, she was ready for that to happen. Maybe it would. Maybe not.

It was just after nine in the morning when Table made it to the tattoo parlor and the sight that hit his eyes made him stop cold. The painted front window had been shattered. Several large bricks were just inside the glass on the display shelf. Police were already there, taping off the damaged area, and the owner was there as well, talking to an officer. Jack spotted Table sitting in his truck and waved him through the police line so he could park in the back lot.

"Fuck me, man," Jack intoned, disbelief in his voice. "Happened sometime yesterday when everything was closed for the holiday. I got insurance and everything, but fuck, what a hassle! No one needs this bullshit!"

Table looked at the destroyed window. What was left of the glass sparkled prettily in the sunlight, and his mouth tightened. "Any equipment stolen or damaged?"

Jack inhaled and blew out a breath. "Naw, man, jus' the window."

Table looked at the storefronts on either side of the parlor. Their display windows were intact. Not a scratch to be seen. "Looks like we're the only ones who got hit. You piss off someone? Sleep with a client's wife or something?"

Jack made a face. "That was only once and a long time ago, man. I ain't done nothing with nobody in so long I'm probably turned back into a virgin."

Table grunted. "Huh, I doubt that." He turned back to view the damage again. "We were targeted. Someone's not happy with us."

"Bad tattoo?"

Table shook his head, "Never had complaints about the work from any of us before. This doesn't look like a bad tattoo job, else they would have fucked up the equipment, not just the window. This was personal for one of us."

A sheriff's deputy chose that moment to approach. "Are you James Boone?"

Table looked at the envelope the uniformed man clutched in his hand. A sense of dread filled his stomach. "Yeah."

"Sorry for this, buddy, especially now during the holidays. You've been served." He handed Table the envelope, turned, and left quickly. Table looked at the white paper rectangle as if it was a snake ready to strike.

Jack pulled out a cigarette and lighter. He tapped one out and placed it between his lips. "You gonna open it?"

Table tore the end off and pulled out the paper inside. His jaw clenched visibly as he scanned the document. "Goddamn fuckin' bitch!" he snarled. "My fuckin' ex-wife is taking me to court, trying to get custody of Angel.

Says she was in a depressive state when she signed away her rights and didn't know what she was doin'. More like she wants the fuckin' money she can get for child support. Fuck!"

Table crumpled the paper and wanted nothing more than to throw it to the ground.

"Think she had somethin' to do with this?" Jack gestured to the destruction.

Table sighed. "It's somethin' she would do, but I can't see her comin' to Asheville to do it. I'm one-hundred percent positive this court shit is for money, and she knows her best chance of gettin' it is hittin' me up in court. She wouldn't have a problem pitching a temper tantrum like this and breaking shit when she didn't get her way, but it don't make sense for her to do it now. Don't matter, since I already know what's gonna happen."

"So you're saying she ain't gonna win this fight?"

Table looked at his friend and boss. "Not a fuckin' chance in hell is that bitch ever gonna take my little girl."

They spent the rest of the day cleaning glass, checking equipment, and nailing two big sheets of thick plywood over the gaping hole. The police had dusted for fingerprints, but that was a token gesture since they had decided it was teenagers making trouble. Table was still not convinced and had a bad feeling about it, but there wasn't much he could do. The crime seemed too directed at them, but Jack was happy with the police assessment and decided to let it be. The insurance adjuster came by and plans were made for the repairs to be done. The parlor would stay closed for the day.

Chrissie showed up, shrugged, and left, texting her friends to meet her at the mall. Jack locked up and went home. Table did the same.

He barely noticed the traffic on the way back to the farm. He'd never expected to hear from Tamara again and he speculated on the reasons why. It had to be money. When she'd left, she had a man with her. Maybe she was on her own again and flat busted broke. She never was good at keeping finances and had left him with a pile of credit card debt he was still paying off. With this new demand, he might be looking at another mountain of debt to pay for another lawyer. Stud had been an attorney at one time and might be able to help, but he wasn't a divorce lawyer and wasn't an expert in family law. He could leave it to the state, but he had already heard plenty of nightmare stories where kids were pulled between the parents like wishbones and the state just about split them down the middle. He did not want that for Angel and would spend every last dime he had to keep that from happening. The trouble was, he was on his last dime. There was no mortgage on the farm, but it was still expensive to run, and with the recent equipment problems there was more money going out than coming in. More than once he'd thought about asking his grandmother to just sell it. She and Carol could move to a high-class retirement village and live out their lives being taken care of, but neither woman would budge. Maybe they were right. Maybe not. But as long as they were physically able to work, they would cling to that plot of land.

He spotted Lori's van parked where it normally was

and noticed his grandmother's old Buick was gone. *Bingo night*, he thought. The crinkle of paper reminded him that the subpoena was in his pocket and he would have to deal with it. Money was going to be a problem and he was unwilling to take any from his grandmother or his club. After the holiday weekend was over, he would be making a few phone calls and seeing what kinds of league fights were happening. He was still registered with the league even though he was inactive. Hopefully, they'd overlook his lack of recent training since at one time he dominated the ring. Fights were not his favorite way of getting money, but it was the quickest and always paid in cash.

With nothing else that could be done, he entered the house.

CHAPTER 9

"You can call down to the VA iffen you need help with the baby. She's sleepin' now, but'll wake up hungry. Bottle's in the icebox and the mashed sweet taters is in the little blue container. You remember how that fancy warmer works. The jackpot's not till nine, but we gots a lotta rounds ta play afore we get to the big money."

Martha and Carol were heading out to paint the town red, or at least mark a few spots. They were loaded with markers and ready for a big night of bingo. Once a month they dressed up as fancy as two old ladies could manage and headed out for a night of revelry, and this month, it just happened to be on the evening of Black Friday.

"Hurry up, Carol! All the good chairs'll be gone afore we get there!" Martha garbled while she painted her mouth with bright red lipstick in the hallway.

"You just want to get a chair next to Floyd Parsons." Carol clacked on the wood floors in wide-heeled sandals with daisies on the closed toes.

Such was the life of two single senior citizens. They got more action than I did these days, but truthfully, I was okay with quiet, solitary nights. Lately, my work days were a blur of constant physical exertion. The need for house cleaners had suddenly exploded and the extra hours of hard manual labor left me exhausted at the end of the day. One advantage was that when I collapsed into bed, I was able to sleep uninterrupted by nightmares all night.

"Floyd done had a crush on me for decades ever since we was in high school. Someday that old coot's gonna make his move, iffen he remembers how. 'Sides, he still has all his own teeth," Martha groused as she put away her lipstick. The orange bubble top she wore clashed horribly, but that was Martha. "Ain't too many our age to choose from these days and Maribelle Mayhew done had her eye on him last month. I heard she brung him some snickerdoodles."

Carol gasped at this bit of news. "Oh my! That hussy!"

I barely contained my laughter. They finally shuffled off and I was left in the house alone with a sleeping baby, a fully stocked kitchen, and a satellite's worth of movie channels. Table had worked the day shift and should have already been home, but he phoned to say something happened and he had to stay at the parlor. I had the whole place to myself. Absolute luxury!

The sun was going down fast while I made dinner for one from the ample leftovers of yesterday's feast. There was no wine available, and I'd had Martha's moonshine experience already. Her blueberry booze was so strong I thought it really would grow hair on my chest. I settled for water. Angel awoke with perfect timing just as I finished washing my dishes. I popped a bottle into the warmer and the mashed sweet potato bowl in the microwave before I went to her room. She fussed a little and rubbed at her eyes with tiny fists as I picked her up. She smelled of sweet baby powder and baby pee. What a combination! She managed to contain her hungry squalls until I had her changed and clean.

She gazed up at me with curiosity as I held her in the crook of my arm and spooned the warmed food into her mouth. I tried not to put too much on the utensil at one time, as whatever she couldn't work around in her mouth she promptly dribbled down her chin. Too late, I remember I was supposed to put on the bib draped over the chair. Both of us were soon covered in sweet potato goop.

"Sorry, Angel. I haven't had a lot of practice," I told her softly. She smacked her lips and reached for my face. "I used to think about babies and children, but I haven't in a while."

I keep talking to her as she practically inhaled the potatoes. I cleaned both of us at the kitchen sink, then went in the living room to watch TV and give her the bottle. You could tell which chair belonged to which sister by the stuff around it. Carol's chair had a knitting basket with colorful yarn, needles, and crochet hooks. An old Bible sat on the table with an adjustable lamp on it. Martha's chair had a Panthers football team throw hanging on the back and a pile of well-read old Harlequin romance novels on her table. I ended up settling us both on the big fluffy play mat on the floor, where Angel promptly showed me her skills of rolling over and skootching. The mat came with soft walls that helped contain the active baby. This was a good thing, as she was starting to explore her mobility and was wiggly. Crawling was definitely on the horizon and the house would need serious baby-proofing.

That's where Table found us.

"The Bobbsey twins not back yet?" he asked, coming into the room. I jumped at the suddenness of his voice. The Netflix movie I'd put on was rolling the credits. I must have slept through most of it, since I could remember only the opening theme.

"Those two will end up shutting down the bingo game. Nanny must be on a winning streak. Either that or she's dancing the night away with one of the widowers." He laughed lightly, his face relaxed and happy but his eyes tired and drawn.

I was disoriented from dozing off. "What time is it?" I asked as I sat up. I looked down at the sleeping baby, still curled up next to me, secured in the play area.

Table squatted next to me and stroked his large hand over the tiny head. "Almost ten thirty. How'd she do tonight?"

He smelled of oil, leather, and man, a combination that was addictive. I inhaled deeply. "She ate a whole bowl of sweet potatoes and almost a whole bottle. Then we played here until we both fell asleep. I think she's really wanting to crawl soon. Martha said something happened at the parlor?"

"Nothing to worry about. Just some teenagers making trouble."

Table smiled and patted his daughter's diaper-covered rump. "That's my girl. Getting ready for another growth spurt, I bet. She's already ahead of the curve in development. Doctor says she'll be tall like her old man."

There was no mistaking the pride in his voice. My heart clenched a bit.

"You know all the stages of child development?"

He blinked. "Not at first. When Angel's mom dumped her on me, I barely knew she existed. I didn't even know she was a she, if you get my meaning. Tamara just came to the bar one night when I was on a date and left Angel, a carrier, and a diaper bag. I was panicked pretty bad, but Betsey and the other ladies helped get me straightened out. Google is a wonderful thing. I spent the first night as a dad looking up all sorts of stuff about babies, how they grow, what to feed them, personal care, lots of shit. I got educated real fast. The second day, I went nomad from the club and came here. Martha and Carol raised me after my mom died. I thought this would be the best home for Angel and me, but I tell you, Lori, I really miss my club."

Nomad? "What do you mean?"

"Means I don't really have a place to call home. The Dragon Runners in Bryson City were my family and my home. I came here 'cause I thought it was best at the time and this was a home. Now, I'm not so sure. I love my grandma and Carol, but living and working a farm is not really me anymore."

Table scooped up Angel and stood tall, signaling for me to do the same with an outstretched palm. I didn't think about it as I placed my hand in his and let him pull me up. The heat brought back the memory of our bike ride.

"Fatherhood. Amazin' how life can throw a curve like a turn on the Dragon's Tail. One minute I'd been on a date and enjoyin' the company of a woman I really liked and was plannin' on getting to know better, and the next minute, I'm googlin' how to change diapers and thinkin' about college funds." He shrugged a shoulder. "I could bitch about it, but it's not going to change anything. I'd rather do somethin' about it, and do it right. I had a good life in Bryson City. Good brothers in the club, boomin' business every day, party every night; only real blight was my marriage fell apart and even through that mess, I had my brothers at my back. I ain't got no regrets 'bout leavin'. I think my daughter is worth it."

A warm, fuzzy feeling bloomed in my middle. "You gave up a lot, Table."

He chuckled lightly and patted Angel's rump again. "Ain't no sacrifice to take care of the people you love. I'd do it again in a heartbeat. I just hope it was the right decision."

He made his way to the back of the house where the baby's room was. I followed since I had nothing else to do but go back to my room. The truth was, I was also intrigued.

"So Angel was a surprise. Did you want children before?" I asked as he swiftly changed the sleeping baby. Angel made a few grunts but didn't wake up.

"Yeah, I wanted kids, but never could imagine them with my ex-wife, 'specially after I found out about her steppin' out on me. Married for less than a month before she was with another man. I tried to keep to the vows I made, but when Tamara kept messin' with other men, I couldn't stay. Didn't even make it a full year before I left. When I took my vows before God and my brothers, I meant every one of them and I kept them solid up until when the divorce was final. I ain't got no stomach for cheats and liars."

The heat in my gut went cold at his words. "I guess I can't blame you for that."

He put Angel down in the white crib. "Yeah, well. It's over and done with. She signed over parental rights without a whimper. Now it's just me and Angel. Tamara named her Angela and that's what's still on her birth certificate, but from the moment I picked her up she became my little Angel. Fits, don'cha think?"

My heart tripped and my head filled with so many thoughts and emotions I could feel my sinuses thrill with the threat of tears. "Yes, it does."

I had to get out of there before the moisture gathering in my eyes spilled over. "I guess I'll leave since you're home. Good night, Table."

My room wasn't too far from the house and I didn't bring a jacket for the short walk. I wrapped my arms around myself in the chill of the night air. When I got to the stairs, I turned and looked back at the house. Table was there in the doorway behind the screen, Angel curled up on his strong shoulder, watching over me. My throat closed as I waved. He waved back and made a shooing motion for me to get inside, and didn't move until I closed my door. I placed my forehead against the cold wood. Only then did I let the tears fall.

CHAPTER 10

I wondered for the fortieth time why I'd let Connie talk me into coming here. Friday night fights at her cousin Julio's gym was not my idea of going out. It had been only a week since Thanksgiving and the mess at the tattoo parlor. I had been working my ass off. Christmas was just a couple weeks away and traffic had doubled as well as my workload. I spent every day cleaning houses, sometimes starting before the sun came up, and helping with Angel every night as Table was either at work or at the gym.

The noise was deafening. Connie and I entered and the wall of sound and were immediately separated by the huge number of people moving in streams around each other. Sweaty bodies packed the gym, concentrating around the central ring. I looked for Connie, but she had long disappeared into the screaming crowd. I was by myself. The feeling of panic crept up the back of my throat; the smell of too many men in one room was overwhelming. It was all I could do to keep from freaking out. The air was like a roasting-hot oven and it was getting harder to breathe. I needed to get out and get some clean air before I choked to death or had a panic attack and started pushing and shoving people. I managed to maneuver through the crowd, and by some miracle found myself at the back of the room in a clearer space. I climbed on one of the risers and got a bird's-eye view of the combatants in the ring. I gasped as one of them was Table.

I found myself getting heated for another reason.

He was magnificent. I'd seen him without a shirt before but not like this. Not when he was covered in a sheen of sweat, his colorful tattoos glowing with life, his muscles defined and bulging with effort, and looking like a hard marble statue of a Greek god. The rings in his nipples had been removed, probably for safety reasons. His hands were covered in some sort of fighting gloves and his face looked a little distorted from the mouthguard clenched between his teeth. His opponent was also large and muscle-bound but nowhere near the perfection of Table.

The roar of the crowd became insignificant as I watched, mesmerized at the sight of the two gladiators. The bell had already rung. The opponent moved and bounced constantly, looking like an overeager kid in comparison to the rock-solid stance Table held. He jumped and waved at the crowd, flipping his arms up, inciting more and more noisy cheers as Table patiently stayed put. It was as if Table was waiting for the man to finish his posturing and preening so the match could really start. The bouncing man finally settled and rushed in to engage Table with a wild lunging swing.

Table ducked and tagged the man in the ribs, hard enough he staggered and almost lost his footing. This made the man angry and his swings got wilder. Table simply continued to duck and punch, different parts of his opponent's body. Ribs, face, chest—wherever there was an opening, Table's gloved fist landed.

Even though I was in the back of the room, I could see the action clearly from my perch. Table looked like a dancer, smoothly controlled in his movements and clearly superior to the lumbering ox he was battling. I found myself silently cheering for him every time he dodged or landed a hit. At one point he was facing me and he looked up and caught my gaze. There was an instant connection. It was like a bolt of electricity hit me and I reeled back, nearly falling from the power. My heart sped up with the intensity of his gaze, and I was burning from the inside out. I had the urge to run, but I couldn't move.

The opponent took advantage of Table's lapse in attention to slam a fist into his face, and Table's head snapped to the side. I gasped as he staggered. The strike didn't seem to faze him much; in fact, Table's face went dark with anger and he came back with a series of strikes that drove the ox back into a corner. One uppercut connected and the man went down in a heap.

The crowd went wild, roaring and chanting, "Tay-ble! Tay-ble, Tay-ble!" He spat out the white mouth guard he wore and launched himself out of the ring. I watched, still unable to move, his eyes locking me in place. The crowd parted as he strode toward me, his focus clear. He put one foot on the bottom riser and reached for me, pulling me down into his body.

"What the fuck are you doing here?" His heat radiated around me as he all but carried me through the crowd. I could tell he was angry, but he still protected me from the well-wishing people slapping his back and arms.

"I came with Connie, but we got separated." He smelled of sweat, but it wasn't offensive. I had the urge to burrow deep into that scent and not come out.

"Yo, Ditch! Connie's in here somewhere. And find Julio. The asshole I just fought had cement in his gloves. Someone's running a fuckin' game!"

"Fuck, I'm on it."

I found myself in a plain locker room, no windows and gray-painted cement block walls. His foot swept the door shut with a bang and muted the crowd noise, already rising for the next match. He was breathing hard as he ripped off his gloves and tore at the bindings underneath. My belly surged at the up-close sight of his perfect body. My breasts tightened and I flushed from head to toe with warmth.

"I repeat. What the fuck are you doing here? These fights are dangerous, especially for a lone woman."

"I was with Connie and—"

"Connie is Julio's sister. No one's going to bother her here. You, on the other hand, are fair game."

I wasn't about to tell him about my earlier panic. "I'm fine."

He leaned in close and I was frozen in place by his intensity. "You're lucky. In the mood I'm in right now, if someone had touched you, they'd be carrying their teeth home in a bag."

"You're bleeding."

His thumb came up to swipe the red trickle from the cut on his cheek. "Yeah. That fucker was trying to hedge his bets by loading his gloves. Too bad for him I got more motivation."

His mouth came down on mine. I tasted the salt of his sweat on his lips as he pressed me close to his slick chest, engulfing me with his heat. I clung to his shoulders and let the storm of feelings wash over me. His kiss went even hotter as his tongue probed at my lips, demanding entry. I opened for him and he dove inside, taking more. His hardness ground against my lower stomach and I reveled in the sensation, moaning into his mouth, ready to explode.

Then panic hit me.

It raced up through my body, paralyzing and choking me. I started struggling, desperate to get free. I couldn't breathe. I tore my mouth away from his and starting clawing at his arms, his head, his face, anything I could reach. I wanted to scream but my throat was filled with black terror and I couldn't.

Table spun me around so my back was against his front, and his back hit the row of lockers with a metallic crash. He easily subdued my fighting body, crossing and pinning my arms in front of me and holding me tight and still with his strength.

"Easy, baby, easy," he crooned in my ear. "Ease up, sweetheart, it's just me. It's only me. I ain't gonna hurt you."

He repeated the endearments over and over again as I grew tired and finally relaxed against him. No, he wouldn't hurt me. He was Table, the man who fixed stuff around the house, the man who took care of his mother, the man who left his brotherhood in order to raise his daughter, a man I could trust.

My throat closed and my sinuses flooded as tears gathered in my eyes. Table's grip loosened but his still held me close.

"Some asshole caused you pain, didn't he?"

I couldn't answer. I was hanging on by a thread of control. My instinct was to run. Fight and run. Keep running and never stop.

Tears flowed from my eyes and I let them fall unchecked. If he let go of me, I'd collapse into a sobbing mess on the floor.

He kept talking.

"I wish I could get five minutes alone with the bastard that did this to you, sweetheart. I can guarantee, he'd never do it again."

That did it. I let it go and cried. It was cathartic, cleansing some of the fears of the last few years of my life. Table slid down the concrete wall to sit on the floor, still holding me in his arms and surrounding me with his solidity. He murmured more words in my ear. "It's okay, baby. You're fine. I got you." Later, I would think about how I'd found myself on the cement floor of a smelly locker room, cradled in the lap of a man who was essentially my landlord.

"I'm so, so sorry." My throat was sore and my voice had

lowered to a gruff-sounding growl.

"Nothin' to be sorry for, sweetheart. It's me who owes you an apology. I got no right to jump you like that. I came on too strong and I shouldn't have. I've been wantin' a taste of you for a while now and with my adrenaline running high I just grabbed for it. I was wrong. This don't mean I'm not interested. I still am, but I know now I gotta handle you with extra care. I hope you know, I'd sooner die than lay a hand on you to cause you pain. I ain't that kinda man and never will be. You have my blood oath to God on that."

I stayed where I was, surrounded by his arms and listening to his voice wash over me. My sobs dried to hiccups. Table didn't make fun of my sounds. He just sat on that nasty floor and held me. I knew he had more questions, but thankfully he didn't ask. I wasn't ready to answer.

A sharp knock on the door caught both of us off guard and we scrambled to our feet. Ditchdigger marched in with Connie, followed by a short Hispanic man who was clearly her brother.

"Damn, brother. You were right about the gloves. Not cement, just some rolls of quarters stuffed in at the knuckles for weight. You're lucky the fucker didn't break your damn jaw." Julio stepped forward and held out a wad of bills. "I run a clean game and that bullshit don't fly in my gym. His ass is disqualified and he ain't comin' back. You get his share as well."

"Thanks."

"*Chingada*, Lori! I'm so sorry! I went looking for Julio and lost you in the crowd. Stupid *pendejos*! Are you okay?

"Yes, I'm fine. Table got to me quick enough."

Ditchdigger laughed. "Damn straight he did. Even with that cheatin' mo-fo! Knocked him the fuck aaoout!"

"If y'all are 'bout finished, I need to get showered off and home. 'S been a long ass day as we still got work in the morning."

Ditchdigger flung an arm around Connie. "All right, brother. We'll leave you to your girl here. I'm guessing you'll take her home with ya?"

"I've got my truck, so yeah."

Table didn't want to let me out of his sight, so I stayed just to the outside of the half wall separating the shower stalls from the rest of the locker room. My eyes followed the stream of water as it poured over his shaved head and wide shoulders and ran down the colorful tattoos on his arms and back. I had to focus my attention on the dingy tiles of the shower room, so I wouldn't stare at him and maybe see something I wasn't ready to see. Not his cock. His eyes. I was afraid of what might be in them. It helped that the shower in the locker room looked just as nasty as the rest of it and I had the urge to fetch my brushes and an economy-sized bottle of Tilex. Still, Table's clean male scent floated to me when he led me to his vehicle and held my elbow while I climbed in. The quiet in the truck was broken only by the whoosh of the road and the click of the turn signal. The tension was thick and growing in me with every mile we drove. Table's silence was troubling, and I imagined he was processing what he thought had happened to me. I hadn't acknowledged it and wasn't ready to share just yet. There was more to it and there were complications. Ones I couldn't share with anyone. Maybe not ever.

The farm was a welcome sight and I felt a great sense of relief when we pulled up the driveway. Table put the truck in park and shut off the engine.

"I'm not going to push you to tellin' me your story, baby girl. I just need to know if you're okay right now."

He had taken off his seat belt and turned to face me in the cab. I could see the glint of his eyes in the low light glow of the dusk-to-dawn lamp pole on the property. His question was an easy one.

"Yes, I'm okay. I'm sorry I panicked at the fight earlier. You probably wouldn't have gotten hurt if I hadn't."

He shook his head. "Not the fight, Lori. Me. Are you okay with me?"

That one was harder. I raised a finger to my lower lip, thinking about his kiss in the locker room. It had been brutal and hard, but up until I panicked, I was into it. His taste, the rough texture of his tongue as he touched mine, the memory of it was just as vivid now as if it was happening again. I didn't know what it meant for us in terms of what we were or what we were going to be now, but I answered him honestly. "I'm okay with you. I can't promise I won't have this kind of anxiety attack again, but I can tell you that I'm not scared of you."

He relaxed a little and leaned back into the seat. "Good enough for now. If you ever do feel scared of me, somethin' I'm sayin' or doin', you just tell me and I'll do my best to stop it and not do it again."

I felt more tears rise in my eyes. "You're a good man, James Boone."

"Come here, Lori."

I scooted over as best as I could and curled under his outstretched arm. He just held me as we sat in silence a few minutes. I suppose the quiet can be intimidating for some people, giving them the need to fill the void with some sort of sound. Sitting under Table's firm muscled arm and being next to his beating heart was enough for me. I could have stayed there all night.

"You gonna be okay up in your room or do you want to sleep in the big house tonight? I can give you my room and bunk on the couch. No trouble."

"I'll be fine in my own space, Table. Thank you for the offer."

"You sure?"

"Yes, I'm sure."

I stifled a giant yawn as I spoke.

"Better get up to bed then, baby girl. You know Martha will be up with the chickens and bellowing for you to get to the breakfast table."

I smiled as we separated and got out of the truck.

He walked me to the steps of my room and stopped.

"It's takin' everything in my power to let you go up those steps by yourself, Lori. I want you to know that. I really want you to be in the house tonight, 'cause I got this urge to keep watch over you right now. It's in my blood to protect people and I can feel it deep that's what you need. I'm also really attracted to you as a woman and I'm scared

I'm gonna push you away if I try to guard you too hard. I'm not real sure what to do about it."

His blunt honesty was making me want to take him up on his offer, but I knew I would be playing a dangerous game with him. If I went to his bed, I may not want to be there alone. He said he would sleep on the couch, but the thought of being next to him, his body heat surrounding me, was very tempting. The invitation would be just sleeping side by side, but that intimacy might make me want even more. That would eventually send him running away from me, angry and bitter. He said once that love died with betrayal and I believed him.

"I'll be fine, Table. I'm not scared of anything here and I'm not running. I promise, if I get that way, I'll call your phone or come into the house on my own."

He looked into my eyes for a long moment and then nodded. "Get on up and lock the door. I'll wait for a bit."

I paused as he stayed at the foot of the steps, watching me get to my safe place as he had several times before. I waved and went into my room, clicking the lock behind me. After brushing my teeth, washing and moisturizing my face, I slipped into the bed and fell into a dreamless sleep. The first one in a long time.

CHAPTER 11

If anyone had told me if I would still be in Asheville for Christmas, I would have said they were out of their minds. Instead, I found myself sitting down for a whole fried turkey and other foods that were almost a repeat of the Thanksgiving meal. The difference was that the attendees to this holiday feast were only Martha, Carol, Table, Angel, and me. The tree was artificial because Carol had a huge fear of the lights causing a fire, but the ornaments were ones collected over the years from the sisters' children and grandchildren. Carefully preserved strings of painted rigatoni pasta, paper angels with stickers on them, photos in frames made from Popsicle sticks, and many others decorated the wiry branches. I thought it was more beautiful than any of the color-coordinated designer trees I'd seen before.

Most of the presents under the tree were for Angel. It was the practical stuff, like a case of diapers, more clothing, but there was also a gigantic teddy bear that was bigger than even me. I wasn't sure what was in Table's mind when he showed up earlier this week with that monstrosity, but I was sure he'd turned a few heads when he drove through town with it sitting behind him on his bike.

I got Angel a set of plastic teething keys, but that was it. The sisters and Table insisted they didn't need anything and didn't do a lot of gift exchanging because of it, but they did have a few token presents for each other. Carol received a fancy cover for her Bible that had handles on it so she could carry the book like a purse. Martha got a new set of waders for splashing around in the creek. Table got a necklace made from a silver angel charm on a leather cord. He put it on, and Angel, who was sitting in his lap, immediately cooed and reached for it.

He had a big grin on his face when he handed me a small green paper bag. "Here you go, Lori. I ain't much on paper wrappin' and these two have been exchanging and re-exchanging the same gift bags for years."

I wasn't expecting anything, but when I pulled out a nice pair of lined leather gloves, I felt my heart catch in my chest. My murmured *thank you* didn't seem adequate enough at the thoughtfulness behind the present.

"So what are yer plans for New Year's? You headed up t' Bryson City?"

Martha's voice could cut through steel if she directed it right.

"I plan to. Betsey's been yammerin' at me to bring the baby up to see her. I've been wanting to take some time there as well. I got some things I need to talk to Brick about."

"You should take Lori along. She ain't been anywhere since she got here. It's nice to have young people around us old farts, but time is y'all need to get out and do stuff with other young people."

Table barked a quick laugh and shifted Angel closer so she could play with the charm without pulling his neck. "You just want to have your own wild party here."

"Damn straight, and having my grandson and great-granddaughter around is gonna cramp my style. I might wanna get one a them bubblin' cajoojee things and go chunky dunkin'."

"What are you talkin' about?"

"Well, we're all too fat to be skinny dippin', so's the next best thing is chunky dunkin'."

The look of horror on Table's face was priceless.

"I could have spent the rest of my life without that picture in my head."

I couldn't help but laugh.

"So what do you say, Lori? Big plans for New Year's, or would you want to come spend it with me and Angel and the best people I know?"

It didn't take long before I found myself traveling with Table.

Table talked about the people at this place we were going and I felt like I knew them before we set foot at the clubhouse he referred to as the Lair. His description didn't do it justice. It was set high on top of a hill, hidden from the main road, and looked like a private resort lodge. Two stories of log cabin, a large parking area, several outbuildings that looked like garages or work areas, and scattered camping cabins were around the property. There was a gated private road to get there. I was glad for Table's truck, as I didn't think my van could handle the steep grade.

We pulled up to the front and a redheaded woman in a puffy blue parka came clattering out of the front door in high-heeled boots. I held my breath, expecting her to slip and fall, but she seemed to be an expert in balance.

"Lord have mercy, Table! It's so good to see you, darlin'." She threw her arms around Table's neck and squeezed briefly. "All right, you done had your hug. Now gimme that baby!"

Table's face broke into a big happy smile. "Jesus, Betsey, can't you wait until I get the road off of me?"

She blew out a *pshhhht* sound and flipped a leather-gloved hand at him. "I done waited long enough. That drive ain't much to get any road on you."

Table's head flew back in a long hard laugh. "Well, come on then and meet my girls."

Two more women appeared on the front porch and he greeted them with a wave. "Hey, Tambre, hey, Molly! Good to see you!"

"Well lookie what the cat done dragged home!"

All three women were dressed in heavy coats against the chill. Table pulled out the carrier that held the now awake Angel from the back seat of the truck. She screwed up her face and rubbed a cloth-covered hand over her eyes. I could tell she was gearing up for a squalling protest.

I went to get some of our luggage from the truck's bed,

but the red-haired woman called Betsey stopped me.

"No need, darlin'. We got prospects for that." She motioned to two strapping young men to come move the stuff we'd brought into the lodge. "I still got a lot of baby stuff from my grandkids, so you ain't gotta worry about a crib and linens and such. I got a couple of them fold-up strollers and a bouncy chair too. You'll be set for a spell. Come on in and I'll show you around."

We shuffled onto the porch and I entered the Lair for the first time. The main room was cavernous with lots of inviting couches where several people were playing video games on a big flat-screen TV. A few others were playing pool on a full-sized table over in a large windowed alcove to the side. There was a built-in bar area and behind that, I could see what I thought was a large kitchen. An open loft overlooked the spacious room from the second floor. I wasn't sure what to expect from a biker clubhouse, but this wasn't it. The people scattered about the room were smiling and welcoming Table back into the fold as if he had never left. The whole place was permeated with a rare, open friendliness that I had not experienced in a very long time. It didn't feel like a club. It felt like a home.

A large and slightly rounded older man approached us, and the others moved away respectfully. This could only be Brick, the man who was the club president and in charge of this group. His aura was one of controlled power, commanding, but not in such a way as to make me afraid. He walked up to Table and the men regarded each other in silent communication.

"Welcome home, son." Brick stuck out a hand and Table grasped it. "Good to see you back."

"Good to be back. More than you think."

They hugged with hard back slaps and I saw a piece of the brotherhood Table had talked about. Brick was more than happy to have Table back in the fold. Apparently, Betsey was as well.

"All right now, you done had your male bonding. Quit stallin' and gimme!"

Angel was alert and curious as Betsey cradled her. She had her father's beautiful brown eyes and regarded Betsey with a wrinkled brow. Apparently she decided Betsey was a good person, as she treated the woman to a big toothless grin and immediately grabbed a handful of bright red hair to stuff into her baby mouth. Betsey just laughed and gibbered at the tiny child.

Other Dragon Runners came to meet us. Table stood by my side, and when so many of his friends appeared, he placed his arm around my shoulders, pulling me close, giving me the comfort and security of his body.

"I got your old room ready for you, darlin'," Betsey mentioned as she detangled her hair from Angel's grip. "Cody's old crib is set up in the upstairs apartment with me. I can have some prospects move it to your room if you want, but it's gonna be awfully tight in there."

Table grinned. "You just want to play grandma, don't cha?"

"Damn straight, darlin'. 'Sides, this way you can get some privacy with your girl, right?"

Table's lips tightened for a moment. "Lori may want her own space. You got a spot?"

Betsey blinked. It was clear she had made the assumption I would stay with Table. I wasn't sure what to expect, but it was a bit of a shock to me that I didn't mind.

"Stud 'n' Eva ain't here too often no more. I'm sure you can use his room if you want."

"I appreciate anything you got to help us out, Betsey. I knew I could count on everyone. It's sure as hell great to be home again."

Betsey's eyes shone briefly before she became all business. "Alrighty then! Sleeper 'n' Max, get them bags where they go and move Table's truck to the garage lot. I 'spect he wants to unload his own bike from the trailer, but take care while you're moving it. Donna, go get some food ready."

She expertly jiggled the baby while she barked out orders, and the people around her scurried to obey. I heard Table's light chuckle.

"Come over here, Lori. Let's you and me sit a spell. You need to meet Tambre an' Molly. The other ladies will be here later for the party."

"Shit," Table muttered under his breath.

Betsey evidently heard him anyway. She whirled to face us. "Course there's gonna be a party! One of our own has come home! Ain't gonna be a wild free-for-all, but we're gonna have us a homecoming celebration with just the club family and the prospects. No hangarounds or others tonight."

My stomach fluttered with dread at being around that many people at once. Table must have felt my thoughts, because he squeezed my shoulder to get my attention. "You okay with this?"

His concern over my anxiety meant more than he knew.

I took a breath. "Yes, I'm okay, I think. It's just a lot to take in and I'm not sure about all this yet."

He leaned in to press his lips to my hair, and his unique scent blend of leather, cologne, and man wafted to my nostrils. I breathed in a lungful.

"Yeah, a lot has happened and I'm sure as shit that more is comin', but you can trust me, baby girl. You're in the best hands in the world right now."

Brick made a humphing noise. "A word, Table." It wasn't exactly a question.

Table nodded again and released me. "You go on with Betsey and the other ladies. They'll take care of you and get you settled. I'll catch up with you in a while." He leaned in and kissed me again, this time on my forehead, before letting me go completely.

The places he touched me tingled as I followed Betsey to one of the sitting areas. She sat on one end of the couch and propped Angel in front of her. "Who's a pretty girl? Who's a pretty girl?" she crooned as the two other women took their places near her. I sat in an overstuffed chair across from all three of them, feeling like I was being set up.

"Table tells me you been helping around his gramma's farm for a while. I met Martha once years ago when Brick was helping get the Asheville chapter set up. That woman is hard as nails and soft as butter at the same time. She'd give you the shirt off her back in a heartbeat but still give you grief for getting yourself to where you need it. I liked her a lot. She done real good when she raised Table."

Molly's blonde curls bounced as she plopped down next to Betsey. She made a few faces at Angel, sticking out her tongue and wrinkling her pert nose.

"Table's a helluva man. My old man, Cutter, thinks the world of him. Says there's no one more trustworthy and the best man to have at your back when you need someone."

Tambre was sitting on Betsey's other side in a chair matching to mine. She reached a finger to Angel, who promptly grabbed it and tried to shove it in her mouth.

"She's cutting teeth soon." Her quiet aura was peaceful and self-assured. This was a woman who knew her worth and was comfortable in her own skin. All the women around me seemed to be that way. I envied them a bit.

"I remember when my first grandbaby, Michelle, started cutting teeth. Lord, have mercy, that child fussed! Chewed on everything! I think my left shoulder stayed wet for a month 'cause she drooled on it so much!" Betsey laughed and jiggled Angel. The baby let out a belly laugh and waved her arms in the air.

"Table's a good daddy." Molly blew a raspberry and earned another baby laugh.

"He's a great artist too. Have you seen his work?" Tambre chimed in.

I shook my head.

"You need to see some of his drawings. They're just

beautiful! Did you know he was the biggest tattoo guy around here before he moved to Asheville? Folks is still callin' for him down at the Dragon's tattoo place over near the soap store on Main. He ran the place for us and we still cain't find no one as good as him. I know Brick would love it if he moves back and takes over again."

Molly placed her hands over her face and proceeded to play peek-a-boo with the delighted Angel. "What about the farm? 'S been in his family a long time, right?"

Betsey let out a *pshhhht*. "I know he inherits a piece of it, but he's said before, he don't want it. He's got a cousin who's interested in keeping it going and Table's plans were to sell his part to him. At least that was his plan before this little one came along. I still can't believe the gall of that woman! Dropping her baby off like that at a biker bar! Table told you what happened, Lori?"

It took me a moment to realize Betsey was addressing me. "Yes. Yes, he did."

She nodded and went back to playing with Angel. "Good riddance, I say. That bitch never deserved a man like Table."

For the next thirty minutes or so, I was regaled with stories of everything wonderful about Table. I had thought when I sat down that the women would be putting me through an inquisition of sorts, but instead it seemed they were determined to sell me on Table and all his goodness. It was a little over the top and I was getting uncomfortable when the subject of their discussion appeared.

Table came up to me and sat on the arm of the chair, leaning down and looking into my eyes. "Tired, baby girl?"

Yes, I was tired. Bone deep tired. I nodded and leaned my head against his waist.

"I'm gonna take Lori to her room for a break. Betsey, can you take Angel for a bit?"

Another *psssht* hissed out. "You don't ever gotta ask me to take care of your young'un, darlin'. Go take care of your girl. I got this."

Table stood up and offered me a hand. I followed him down a long hallway of rooms. He pointed out one on the way. "This one is mine. You're welcome to come and go as you please if you need or want to."

He showed me to a corner room at the end of the hallway. It was larger than I expected with a neatly made-up queen size bed covered in a beautifully sewn quilt. An ornate dresser with matching desk and nightstand were other pieces of furniture, and my few bags were already in the room, sitting in front of a small futon sofa.

"Bathroom is over there. No tub, just a shower, but it looks like there are plenty of towels. Probably Eva's doing. I bet the bed quilt is one of hers as well."

I was overwhelmed. The easy acceptance into this group was something I had never experienced. All my life, I had been treated either as a porcelain doll or as an accessory. These people didn't know me except through Table, and his knowledge was still limited. I felt the sting of tears in my eyes.

"It's beautiful. Everything. It's just...."

He enfolded me in his arms and I clung to him, taking in his scent of leather and man.

"Ain't no one here gonna hurt you, baby girl. I'd trust these people not just with my life, but with Angel's too. No better mama hen than Betsey. Whatever it is, you can let it go for a bit."

That sounded like a good plan to me. I could relax and just be in the moment. It was about to become a new year and one full of new possibilities. I stretched out on the bed after Table left and closed my eyes, thinking of the freedom of the bike ride I had shared with him weeks ago. Hopefully soon, that freedom would truly be mine.

CHAPTER 12

Table was right. I'd never seen so many people at a gathering acting so free and confident. The Lair was filled with laughter, joking, food, and drink. There were people playing pool in some sort of tournament, and I noticed Table was ranked at the top. Others were playing video games. Kids were running around, threading their way through the adults like they were running an obstacle course. A few half-hearted *slow downs* were called out but for the most part ignored.

Betsey had the place running like a well-oiled machine. Every detail, from tables, cloths, and cutlery to the coolers full of beer, was covered and ready. Large trash cans were in place for the aftermath when everyone would be stumbling around in a food coma. After a brief rest, I helped Betsey and several of the other club wives in the big kitchen with celebration preparations. Despite the cold weather, some of the prospects had already set up several turkey fryers on the outside deck, and others had been manning a gigantic black smoker that held an entire pig. It had been cooking all day and the luscious smell of barbecue wafted its way indoors.

My job was peeling potatoes along with the woman named Donna. I wasn't sure about her place in the club, as she wasn't a wife or an "old lady," but somehow she seemed to belong. At least she belonged enough to complain about the work.

"I cain't see why we hafta peel and cook forty pound of taters from scratch. Instant is faster. Don't take no time at all to boil some water and stir 'em up."

This was obviously the wrong thing to say to a woman organizing a huge family party. Betsey whirled around, Angel firmly anchored over one shoulder, and sent such a fiery look at Donna, I thought the woman would be incinerated on the spot.

"Ain't no way, no how, this Southern woman is gonna serve instant potatoes at a family gathering. I ain't never fixed 'em in my life and I ain't startin' now."

Silently, I agreed with Donna, but I also understood Betsey's pride in what came out of her kitchen. I had finished peeling one ten-pound bag of potatoes and was starting on the next one when Table came into the kitchen. He stopped next to me and stole a chunk of the vegetable. He popped it in his mouth and crunched down. I grimaced at the thought of eating raw potato, but apparently that was acceptable here.

"You okay, baby girl?"

"Yes, I'm fine."

He nodded and looked up at Betsey. "Any chance I'm

gonna get my little girl back anytime soon?"

"Nope. Now get outta my kitchen. No, wait. Go check on them chafin' dishes I tole Bruiser to set up a while ago."

"What the hell is a chafin' dish?"

"It's the one that's got the little pots of fire you put under 'em to keep 'em warm. Now scoot!"

Table glanced down at me when Betsey turned her back and rolled his eyes.

"I heard that!"

My mouth burst into a wide smile as Table grabbed another chunk of potato and bolted. More and more, the appeal of this group of people was getting to me. Their acceptance and openness was genuine and the affection between them was contagious.

Later that night, I watched as Table won the friendly pool tournament with a complicated banking trick shot. I heard the cheer and saw the heavy back slaps as he collected a few bills from those wagering against him. I was lounging on one of the many couches, a delicious margarita in my hand and a light buzz in my head. Angel was fast asleep up in Betsey's private area. Table and I both had been up to check on her several times during the evening. She must have been exhausted from the excitement of the day, because she went down without a whimper.

Table came up behind me and sat on the couch arm. He took the drink from my hand and sipped at it. His face wrinkled up.

"Damn, Lori. How in the hell can you drink this girly sweet shit?"

I pouted at him and grabbed my drink back. "It is not girly. It's good."

"It's girlie."

"No, it's not."

"Yes, it is."

I rolled my eyes and raised my nose in the air as high as it would go. "You're such a… such a… man!"

He barked out a laugh. "That, baby girl, we definitely agree on."

Several of the club prospects were carrying trays loaded with full shot glasses. I guessed it was tequila, as they also carried lemon wedges and salt shakers. One of the members salted his thumb before picking up a shot and a lemon.

"Almost midnight! Let's bring in the new year Dragon style."

What the hell, I thought. I'd never tried drinking a shot before, but in the past year I'd done many things I hadn't in my previous life. Table picked up a shaker, salted his thumb, and handed it to me. I copied his every move, including the way he held the lemon with his salty hand and the shot glass with his other.

Someone started counting down.

"Ten… nine… eight…"

The excitement was palpable. What was it about a new year that was so rousing? Maybe the idea of renewal, second chances, or starting over. Whatever the concept, I was in the zone.

"Seven… six… five…"

I looked at Table and I could feel my face radiating the

elation of the moment.

"Four… three… two… one…"

His head descended and he kissed me. Soft. Gentle. Sweet. The tip of his tongue danced over my lips, sending thrills running through my body. I was so lost in his touch, I scarcely heard the cries of Happy New Year. He pulled back slowly, ending the kiss.

"Happy New Year, baby girl."

I watched mesmerized as he licked his thumb, threw back the tequila, and bit into the lemon. His eyes stayed on mine the whole time and the intensity of that gaze had waves of heat pulsing over me. I didn't break the stare as I repeated his movements. Salt. Shot. Lemon. *Oh shit!* A different heat invaded my body. One that scorched a path from my esophagus to my stomach. I choked and coughed, my eyes watering like crazy and my nose filling up to start running.

"Oh, jeez! Oh my! Water! Ice!"

I had to give Table credit for trying not to laugh at me. I was sure he still remembered my reaction the first time he did that, when I ran into the spider web. When he couldn't hold it in any longer, it burst from him in long peals that nearly sent him to the floor. He managed to snag a bottle of water from a passing prospect and hand it to me before he had to sit or fall over.

"Damn, baby girl. First time takin' a shot?"

"Yeah. Was it that obvious?" The croak exacerbated the burn in my throat, and I gulped at the water.

"No, not at all," he deadpanned, before going off in gales

of laughter again. I did my best to ignore him, but that was impossible. His mirth at my expense didn't feel cruel or demeaning. It was just Table enjoying the moment.

It wasn't too much longer until the stresses of the day finally caught up to me. Or maybe it was me not being used to so much booze. My head was pleasantly buzzing as Table walked me back to the room I was using and stood in the doorway. He stroked one finger down my cheek.

"You gonna be okay for the night, Lori?"

I blinked, suddenly sleepy. "Yeah, I'm good."

He leaned in and gave me a sweet lip touch. "Sleep well, baby girl. We gotta travel back tomorrow."

He waited another few seconds before turning and walking away. I sensed he didn't want to but needed to.

My heart was falling for this man and my body cried out for more than just his kisses, but my head was holding back. Secrets, so many secrets! I was at a crossroads and didn't have a clue which road to take. Did I let this man into my heart? Did I risk giving him a piece of me? A piece I may never get back?

CHAPTER 13

Connie had called me with a wretched feverish voice and pleaded with me to take on the cleaning jobs for a few days solo. Anita was out of town with her boyfriend for the weekend, so what could I say? During the holidays, the cleaning and house primping jobs had picked up huge and I was stashing away a huge wad of money. The work seemed to increase after the holidays simply because of the cleanup effort involved. It was nice making so much extra, but I was getting sick of taking down ornaments, wrestling strings of lights down from gutters, and removing whatever else the matron of the house had put out as Christmas decorations. I had always loved primping up for the holidays and getting into the Christmas spirit, but after wrestling the sixth gigantic formerly live tree to the curb for pickup, I was over it.

Since it was just me working through the houses, it took me longer than usual. A few of the women were miffed that their schedules were interrupted by my vacuuming and dusting for them, but most of them were okay with the delays and the later hours. I finished my last house around seven thirty and was finally on the way home, smelling of a combination of Pine-Sol and bleach. Thick flakes had fallen heavily throughout the day. It had stopped earlier but left a coating on the trees and lawns in sparkling white. It was a beautiful postcard vista. The only ugly bit was my dilapidated van making its way through the pristine snow on the roads.

Eventually the pretty scenery gave way to the twisted hill road that led out of the highbrow community and back down to the city. I still had some distance to go to get home and could already feel the vehicle sliding around. I cursed as the tires lost traction again and again. The hills around this mountain suburb of Asheville were steep and, in some cases, needed four-wheel drive and good tires to negotiate. I didn't have either, so my progress was slow and tedious. I thought the main road should be fine once I got there, but getting there was going to take a long time. A loud honk made me jump and I spotted a dark sedan on my tail. I cursed at the reckless driver, as there wasn't a lot of room for passing on these roads and I wasn't sure what he expected me to do about it. I inched over as best I could and felt the van slip again. I risked the cold air and put down the window to wave the beastly driver around me. He didn't budge but kept right on my bumper, flashing his lights and honking his horn as we coasted down the hill.

"Stupid asshole!" I muttered as I rode the brakes down the steep grade and hoped he wouldn't ram into me. I was starting to feel some genuine fear when he kept pushing.

Just get to the main road, just get to the main road, I thought over and over as I slipped and slid. Was this just some random asshole driver, or was he following me? Trying to run me off the road? Had all my efforts to stay under the radar failed? Maybe I should just take the highway exit once I got there, just abandon my stuff back at the farm and *get away*. There was a loud bang underneath my van and the brake pedal suddenly pushed to the floorboard, not an ounce of pressure. The vehicle picked up speed and there was nothing I could do about it. I screamed as the van skidded, and pumped at the useless brakes. The steering wheel suddenly locked and I wrestled with it, trying to gain some sort of control. The van spun like a mad carnival ride and crashed hard into the guardrail, coming to a complete stop. I was lucky it hadn't given way and sent me over the side of the mountain.

I was shaking like a leaf and my hands were locked onto the worthless steering wheel when the sedan pulled over across the other side of the road. A slim-built man in a thick black parka got out of the car. I couldn't see his face as he slowly approached my van. My throat worked, trying to find my voice, any voice to scream, but I was locked tight in terror. I wanted to leap out of the vehicle and run, but I was frozen to the spot. All I could do was watch and wait.

"Hey, you okay?" came a young male teenage voice. "I hope I didn't scare you none. I's just tryin' to get you to stop. There's somethin' leakin' out the back."

I let out a breath as two more teenagers came out of the

car and stood by my crumpled van. I felt a tingle of relief draw up in my nose and I nearly cried in front of the kids. "Yeah, I'm good," I managed. "My brakes failed."

"I ain't surprised. There's a long line of fluid trailing down the hill for a couple miles. I bet the main line is completely dry. Probably have to get a tow."

"No probably about it. You got two flat tires as well as the bad brakes," the other boy piped in, pointing to the collapsed front end. "This puppy ain't going nowhere."

The first kid whistled at the damage and pulled out a fancy smartphone. "You got a cell? Someone to call?"

I had my cheap throwaway and there was only one person I could call. "Yeah, I do." I grabbed the new phone I had picked up a few days ago and hit one of two numbers I had programmed.

"'Lo?" Table's low voice rumbled in my ear. I could hear music in the background and the buzzing of the tattoo machines.

"Table," I managed to utter before I lost it. I don't know why, but hearing his masculine voice did something to me. Tears poured down my cheeks, and I sucked in a breath, trying to hold back the sobs.

His tone went from inquiring to alert. "Talk to me, Lori. What's happened?"

I couldn't say anything without my breath hitching. The leader of the teenagers took the phone from my hand and spoke into it.

"Hello, this is Bryce Turner. This lady's had an accident 'bout halfway down Briar Cliff Road near the bell curve.

Bad brakes, we think, and two flat tires. Nah, she says she's okay but shaken up a bit. How long? Ah-right. We'll hang till you get here." He closed the phone with a snap and handed it back to me. "Your boyfriend will be here soon. You can sit in the car and keep warm if you want."

I wasn't feeling the cold, but I was still shaking like a leaf. "Not a boyfriend. Just a friend," I stuttered, and wrapped my arms around myself, fighting for control. "It's the adrenaline kicking in from the accident. I'll be fine if you and your friends want to take off."

He looked at me like I was an alien from another planet. "My mom would skin me alive if I left someone alone in the cold and the dark, especially after a car wreck. Our curfew ain't for a few hours and we don't have plans that can't be changed."

"Where would you want to go on a night like this?" I asked. "It seems the bad weather would be enough to keep everyone at home."

He grinned and shrugged. "You grow up in a mountain city, you get used to mountain weather. Heather, Scott, 'n me were headed to the mall for some shopping and Starbucks." He pointed to his vehicle. "I got four-wheel drive, six cylinders, and heavy-duty snow tires on that sucker. Best car for going around in the snow. 'Sides, the biggest problem around here ain't snow, it's ice. Might be that's what you hit on that curve, you know? Black ice? You can't see that shit—uh—stuff, until you hit it."

Heather jumped into the conversation, "You ain't lyin'! My cousin Rowena hit a patch of black ice last year. Totaled her Mazda!"

The kids exchanged tale after tale of car wrecks, bad snowstorms, and other stories while we waited. They were funny and I found myself relaxing in their company, laughing at the outrageous tales. I found out Bryce was a senior in high school, being raised by a single mom and working part-time at a local auto parts store. He was planning on going to college at UNC Asheville next year and was undecided between majoring in Environmental Studies or Atmospheric Sciences. He was definitely the leader of the little group and the most mature kid I'd ever met. I could see a bright future ahead of him.

Their easy banter kept me occupied enough that I didn't notice the time going by. Bryce perked up and pointed out the headlights coming in our direction. I was surprised to see a tow truck and two other vehicles driving and parking on the narrow shoulders. I recognized Table's truck as he stopped just behind Bryce's car. He got out, slammed the door closed, and stalked over to me.

"Table," I was able to say before he clutched me to his chest in a big bear hug. I had no choice but to hug him back.

"Damn, baby girl," he said raggedly. The warmth of his body seeped into mine, and I realized how cold I had become. I felt those stupid tears start up again and buried my face in his thermal-covered chest. He finally released me. "You okay? Nothing broke? Need a hospital?"

"No, I'm good. Maybe a few bruises, but I'm not hurt." I sniffed and hoped I hadn't left any residue on his shirt. He was wearing his club cut and I belatedly watched as two men from the second truck started hooking up my poor van to the tow truck. They also had on Dragon Runners cuts.

"My brothers. You already know Ditchdigger, and the other one is Chevy. I can't remember if you met him at the bar, but he and Ditch own a top-notch garage. They'll get you sorted. What happened?"

Bryce talked to him, explaining how he'd spotted the line of brake fluid on the road and tried to get me to stop. Table listened intently and kept his arm around me during the entire time. I didn't mind it. Not one bit. The other two kids stared with wide eyes at the biker insignia on the backs of the men handling my van. I saw Bryce glance at the emblem more than once, but not with trepidation. More like longing.

"Thanks for taking care of my girl here. You ever need something, come see me at Asheville Ink."

"I've been thinking about your club and seeing what I'd have to do to join." Bryce's chin boldly rose a notch. "My mom's not real thrilled with that idea, but I've been watching you guys for years. You got a reputation for taking care of your people and I want that for my mom. It's just me and her right now, but I don't know what will happen once I go off to college. I gotta make my own way, you know? It would be a big relief to me, knowing someone was around to watch out for her."

Table dipped his chin in affirmation. "It's not easy getting into the club and not everyone is cut out for club life. You're serious, I can talk to my people. If it's mostly about your mom, you just let me know if she needs somethin' and I'll take care of it."

Table held out a hand and Bryce took it for a man/boy handshake. No, I couldn't say that. This was definitely a man-to-man handshake. Bryce's mom was doing a great job in raising him.

The teens loaded back into Bryce's car and took off.

"Got 'er hooked up and ready, Table," Ditchdigger called out. "Shee-it! It's colder than a witch's tit out here. You owe me a free tattoo!"

Table snorted and turned his attention to the van, now attached to the tow truck. "You still ain't paid for the last session, brother. I'd say we're even."

"I'll pay you back," I jumped in. "You shouldn't be out any money over me."

Table looked at me and gave me his bright smile. "Didn't you hear what the boy said, darlin'? We take care of our people. You're our people. Get it?"

"But I owe you now."

He shook his head. "You don't owe nothin'."

"But Table—"

"Nope. Not goin' there. Get in in my truck, baby."

"I—"

"Truck, Lori."

I rolled my eyes and tried to find my anger, but I was too worn from the workday, too cold from the night, and too mentally numb to argue. The adrenaline was wearing off and I was crashing hard.

"All right, Mr. Bossy!"

Table's head went back and he roared with laughter.

"God Almighty, baby girl! Only you can come up with 'Mr. Bossy'!"

I sniffed and held my head up as I went to his truck and climbed in the passenger side. I sat and watched him talk to Ditchdigger for a few more minutes before he came and got in the driver side. The truck started with a powerful growl and heat poured over my cold face and body. I supposed I could have held on to my pique, but I was happy to be in the warm cab. The thought would occur to me later that calling Table for help had been a natural reaction, and I'd never doubted he would come for me.

CHAPTER 14

The slippery road didn't faze him or the truck at all as he drove the rest of the way into the city. The snow that looked so pretty in the neighborhood was now a slushy mess. It was past nine o'clock and I was fighting sleep with my head against the window, watching the city buildings go by.

"Hungry?" Table asked. "Asheville Pizza and Brewing is still open. Cool place and great food. My treat."

My stomach gurgled at the thought of my missed dinner. I had nothing special back at my room and the thought of hot pizza was appealing. "Sure," I agreed.

"We'll eat, then I'll drop you off at home. I'm still on at work tonight and need to finish out my shift," he planned out loud as he pulled into the parking lot.

I perked up a bit. "You don't have to do that if you're going back to work. I can eat something back at the house so you don't waste any more hours."

He chuckled and turned off the engine. "Lori, babe, look around. There's not a lot of people out tonight and not many are dying to get a tattoo. Most of the business is in the summer when people are showing off a lot of skin. Weekends are pretty steady, but weeknights? Hardly enough people to keep the doors open. Tell you what, we'll eat, then you can come sit with me at the parlor for a bit. If nothin's happening, I'll close up early, 'round eleven, or so and we'll go home then. You need to crash, there's a futon in the back room."

I was too tired and hungry to argue.

Table was right in that the place was a neat restaurant and bar. The movie-themed menu was clever and there was even a movie theatre in the building. We scarfed up a gourmet pizza between us and had a couple of local brews to go with it. The ride to the tattoo parlor was short, and I hit my second wind with a full stomach.

Asheville Ink was in an older building in the downtown area. Artistic sculptures, bright-colored paintings on the sides of buildings, and eclectic boutique stores made up the area. I expected the parlor to be some dingy and dirty hole-in-the-wall place, but upon entering I could tell I was quite wrong. The walls were painted a pale gray with lots of framed art hanging on them. A few frames held newspaper articles on the place, great reviews on the artists that worked there. There was a glass counter that held a wide selection of pierced jewelry pieces and on top were several large binders. The place smelled of rubbing alcohol, disinfectant, and the faint scent of a sandalwood candle trying to combat the two. There was some new age-y music playing over the speakers.

"This is nice. Very professional."

A blue-haired woman with several bars in her eyebrows and a nose ring came out of the back.

"Hey, Table. My last guy canceled just after you left. If you've got this, I'm outta here."

"No problem, Chrissie. Take it easy on your way home," Table said as he took off his leather jacket and knit hat.

"Fuck that!" she retorted, wrinkling her nose. I got a glimpse of her pierced tongue as she spoke. "I know there's a party getting started somewhere." She tapped at her phone and the music stopped. "Laters!"

Table raised a hand as she departed. He took out his phone and swiped the screen. A moment later, slow, soft jazz came over the wireless speaker—another surprise, as I was expecting some sort of loud country music like what was played at A. W. Shucks bar. I'd heard Table play country music before, but apparently he had other tastes as well.

"Best time of the night is when I'm here alone and can play my own stuff," Table remarked as he went to his cubicle. All the workstations were in semiprivate alcoves that could be curtained off as needed. Table's spot had pictures of bikes, artwork around bikes, the Dragon Runners insignia on the wall, and a picture of him and Angel. He was leaning back in one of the recliners at the farmhouse, looking down at his daughter. She was dressed in a pink onesie and was curled up on her daddy's black T-shirted chest, his colorful arms holding her close. My heart skipped a beat just looking at the pure love this rough man had for his little girl. He would walk through fire for her and smile while he was doing it.

"Futon's in the back if you want to crash for a bit. I have to keep the shop open for a while as per the posted hours, but if nothing happens, I'll call the boss to close early. Deal?"

"I want a tattoo," I announced. I was just as shocked as Table, but once I said it, I knew I meant it. Furthermore, I knew what I wanted.

Table looked at me with hooded eyes. "Lori, it's been a tough night and getting a tattoo now might not be the best idea. Not something you decide on when you're not thinking clearly."

"My thinking is very clear right now. I want a tattoo. I want a four-leaf clover on my lower stomach, and I want you to do it."

He frowned and shook his head. "Not a good idea, baby girl. Stomach tattoos can hurt a lot and I'm guessing you don't have any other ink. Bad place to start. Better on the back of your shoulder or calf."

I looked into his eyes and stated as stubbornly and firmly as I could, "I won't be able to see it if you put it there. Please, Table, I'm not scared of a little pain. Believe me, I can take it."

He stared at me for a few more minutes and I nearly lost my nerve. His mouth formed a flat line and he finally nodded. "Okay, Lori. If you're sure. You wanna pick a design or do you want me to draw up something?"

I let out my breath. "Draw up something."

He pulled out a sketchpad and pencils. I watched as he drew and colored in green and gold, a simple but beautiful four-leaf clover surrounded by a Celtic knot. It was small, about an inch in diameter.

"It's perfect. How long will it take and how much?"

Table looked at the drawing. "'Bout an hour, maybe less if you can really take it."

"I can take it," I repeated, determined, climbing on the padded table and pulling up my shirt at the same time. "How much?"

"Work it out in trade later, deal?" Table said as he snapped a pair of blue rubber gloves on his hands. "You need to undo your pants and take them down a bit. Not completely off, though. Just so I can get to the area you want."

I hesitated for a moment. Lying on the table on my back and exposing my stomach put me in a vulnerable position. I looked at Table's face and made the call.

"Trade is good," I affirmed as I undid my jeans and slid them down to my hips. Table wiped across my stomach with rubbing alcohol and I jumped a little at the cold solution. He looked up at my eyes, his face serious. "You can still change your mind. I promise I won't judge."

"I'm not changing my mind. I do want this. I-I kinda need it."

"This clover symbol mean something to you?"

"Yes."

He gazed into my eyes after my firm one-word answer, came to his own decision, and loaded up his tattoo machine with ink. "This is going to sting. Let me know if it gets to be too much and you need a break."

The buzzing noise of the machine started as he placed the tips of the needles on my skin. The pain wasn't terrible at first, more irritating than anything else. But it was constant and became sharper as Table continued to work.

"Have I ever told you about how I got my club name?" Table asked casually, trying to distract me.

"No, you haven't," I bit out, trying to keep still. Table dipped more ink and the machine kept buzzing.

"I used to shoot a lot of pool. Loved the game and played whenever I got a chance. Used to compete some in a few local tournaments but nothin' big like a national competition. It's the strategy and skill that really gets me into it. Knowin' where to hit, makin' a bank shot, how to spin the ball to put it where I want it next, or where to put it to block my opponent. I love that kinda stuff. It takes plannin', patience, and a steady hand. That's somethin' Martha taught me about life in general. You want somethin', you gotta have a plan, you gotta work steady to get it, and you gotta be patient while you're gettin' there. I think that applies to a lot, like the garden, raisin' a kid, bunch of other stuff."

He loaded a different set of needles in the machine and kept going. The burn was more intense and I gritted my teeth but forced myself to stay still.

"I didn't get my road name because I like to play pool. After I got out of the Marines, I traveled around a bit, just me and my bike. Unsettled, you know? I saw some stuff in Afghanistan, not as extreme as some soldiers, but still not a place that makes happy memories. I was playing a tournament up at a bar in Bryson City when this guy started roughin' up his girl. I don't mean just pushin' and yellin' like the asshole you saw over at the bar. I mean he was *roughing*.

He was drunk as fuck and yelling shit at her, calling her all sorts of names, slapping her around. He threw beer in her face and she just stood there taking it. I'll never forget her look. Blank. Like life had completely defeated her. Dealin' with some drunk asshole doesn't bother me a bit, but seeing her? That place she was in scared me."

I stopped feeling the pain of the pulsing needles. My mind was numb to anything but the sound of his voice as he spoke.

"The whole bar stopped to watch the show and this one guy, the bouncer, was comin' over to stop that shit. Big mean-looking guy, as cold as they come. Before he could get to the game area, the guy rears back his fist and let loose a full-power roundhouse on his girl. Blood flies and she goes down hard. Then a bunch of other men started yellin' shit and comin' over, but I was right there when it happened."

He wiped a cloth over my stomach and dipped more ink.

"You know I was raised by my grandma and her sister. The reason is my daddy put my mama in the ground by doing that shit to her when I was a kid. Saw my mom bloodied more than once, but since I was a kid, I couldn't do much about it. I sometimes wonder if she took the beatings so I wouldn't have to. I was in the first grade when I came home to police cars and yellow tape around the trailer we lived in. I can still see them flashing lights and all the uniforms walkin' around. I didn't get to see her or what he'd done to her, but I did see them wheel out the gurney she was layin' on, all covered up in a sheet. I was young, but I wasn't stupid. I knew what had happened. He's somewhere in a prison and will stay there for life. I haven't seen him since then and never care to lay eyes on that fucker again. If I ever do, I'll probably kill him."

His voice was casual even though his words were not. "Anyway, long story short, I broke my best cue stick over that guy's head, flipped his sorry ass on the pool table, and pounded the ever-lovin' shit outta him. I just couldn't stand there and do nothin' while that asshole decided he would beat on his woman. Those other men just watched me for a bit before they pulled me off of him. I went a little too far and thought for sure I was going to jail. The guy I beat up was out cold and tore up pretty bad. That's the night I met the Dragon Runners. I don't know how they handled it, but I was never charged. One man came over to the pool table and was looking down at the guy. I'll never forget what he said. He shook his head and huffed, 'That's gonna stain.' And then he looked up at me, square in the eye, and said, 'That's one way to clear a table.' I've been Table ever since."

He wiped across my stomach again with a cooling gel. "That was Brick. I prospected with the club and became a Dragon Runner about a year later. Nothing more solid than the kind of brotherhood my club has. Don't matter if I'm there or here, they have my back and I have theirs. There's a trust and integrity you won't find anywhere else, and believe me, I've looked. Tattoo is done. Wanna see?"

I took a moment to register what he'd said.

"Done? Already?" I blinked.

"Yup. Mirror's over there. Don't touch, just look."

He helped me off the table and I felt the soreness kick

in. I moved to the full-length mirror and studied my tattoo. The leaves were shaded green and detailed with tiny veins from the center. The knot was in gold and black, and twisted between the leaves, making them appear more defined.

"Beautiful," I breathed.

Table stood behind me and looked at the image in the mirror. "Yes, it is," he said gruffly. He didn't touch me, but his regard set off a flare in my middle that had nothing to do with the tattoo. Impulsively, I reached a hand behind me and stroked his cheek, feeling the growth of his whiskers and the smoothness of his mustache. His gaze intensified, but he still made no move to touch me. It may have been anxiety over the accident, worry about my vehicle situation, the fact I was exhausted from so many work hours in so many days, the pain and thrill of getting this tattoo, or a combination of everything. I didn't know. But I turned around and pulled his mouth to mine. He slanted and kissed me back, running the tip of his tongue gently over my lips, asking for permission, and I opened my mouth to him. He took the invitation and deepened the kiss, his tongue lightly playing with mine. He didn't touch me anywhere, his hands staying rigid by his side, and let me lead. When I ended the kiss, he leaned his forehead against mine and muttered, "Damn, baby girl." Both of us were breathing hard, and that flare in my middle had turned into a smoldering flame. The shock was, I wasn't the least bit frightened of the intimacy. In fact, I actually felt a desire for more. Was I ready for that? Was he offering?

We stood there a few minutes, not moving, just sharing

the space. He finally broke the spell by going to his station and bringing back a wide white piece of gauze, which he swiftly taped over the glistening tattoo. He handed me a pamphlet of instructions on how to care for the tattoo for the next few weeks.

"It's midnight thirty, past time for me to close. You ready to go home?"

It was on the tip of my tongue to flip off something about that being rhetorical, but the depth of his tone told me now was not the time to be cute. I nodded and moved to the door.

The ride home was quiet and my second wind left me with an exhaustion crash I had never experienced before. I was bleary-eyed and nearly stumbling when we reached the farm. Table helped me out of the car and up to the door of my room. I was leaning heavily into his solid body. He kissed my hair as he unlocked my door. "You gonna make it, baby girl?" he whispered against my head.

"Yeah, I'm good. Thank you for everything, Table. You have no idea how much I appreciate you."

He kissed my forehead again. "No problem. You call me anytime, darlin', I'm there. 'Night, Lori. Lock up before you faceplant on the bed. Same deal as before. You get nervous, can't sleep, come on to the big house and take my bed. I'll move to the couch, yeah?"

"Yeah," I said sleepily.

He stayed on the small landing until I clicked the lock shut, and then I heard the squeak of the steps as he went down to find his own bed. I put the pamphlet on the nightstand and stripped off my jeans, letting them drop to the floor. I didn't bother to take off my shirt, just contorted myself enough to unhook my bra and pull it out of my sleeve. My stomach burned from the tattoo, but I had Tylenol. When I dreamed, I saw myself lying in a field of four-leaf clover.

And I was smiling.

CHAPTER 15

"Further mystery surrounds the disappearance of Jeffery and Vivian Townsend. While Mr. Townsend has been allegedly jet-setting around South America, Mrs. Townsend has not been seen since she left with her husband on their yearlong humanitarian tour. The only contact anyone had had with Mrs. Townsend has been through emails authorizing foundation expenditures through Senator Townsend's office that were supposedly for the schools supported through the foundation. We have learned that one of the foundation's schools is on the verge of closing due to lack of funding. We have called Senator Townsend's office multiple times asking to interview Mrs. Townsend, however, his office has told us neither she nor Jeffrey Townsend Jr, can be reached. Both of their social media accounts have been stagnant for months, so the big question today, where is Vivian Townsend?

"Yo, Table-man!" Ditchdigger walked in the tattoo parlor, interrupting the news update on the XM station. More like stomped, as his size made a quiet entry anywhere impossible. "I got yer girl's ride ready."

Table continued to work on the child's face he was tattooing on a client's left pec. "What all was wrong with it?"

Ditch sat heavily on the leather sofa in the waiting area, and the piece of furniture groaned under the sudden weight. "More like what wasn't wrong with it. Head gasket leaking, brake pads at 90 percent worn, rotors chewed and no clearance for turning, tensioner belt going bad, battery with two dead cells and another one 'bout to go. I'm surprised the damn thing even cranked! If it was a horse, it'd be a mercy to shoot it and put it out of its misery. I put in more work than the thing is worth. You owe me big, brother."

Table grunted a short laugh. He wasn't surprised. The van had looked and sounded like it was on its last legs. Ditch was fixing up the van on the sly and wouldn't tell Lori about everything he'd had to do to it. That would be between him and Ditch. Table knew Lori would want to pay for it, and Table was too much of a man to let her do it.

"That's not all I found, brother." Ditch's voice changed, dropping low and sounding serious. "Them tires was rough, but they didn't blow on their own. I found stab marks in 'em, the kind you can only make with a serious-ass knife. And the brake fluid leak? It had some help too. Someone was trying to cause that wreck. You hear any more from your ex?"

Table felt the heat of rage rise up in him. Too many problems had cropped up to be coincidental. The stuff at the farm, the vandalism at the parlor, the sudden change of heart from his ex, and now the deliberate tampering with Lori's van that could've cost her life or someone else's. Table's thoughts raced. His ex wanted money but hadn't done much more than send a court notice. His lawyer had said that in order to reverse her decision at this late date in Angel's life, she would be looking at a long drawn-out time in and out of the courtroom for months, maybe years. This was not like Tamara. The woman he knew would expect a quick buck or two and wouldn't have the stamina or patience for a long court battle. He suspected there was something else going on, as he hadn't heard from Tamara at all, just the court summons.

Something stunk to high heaven and he was getting tired of it.

"I'm getting a fucking bad vibe here, Ditch. This shit is too much on top of everything else."

"My spidey senses are telling me this ain't nothing to do with your ex. She ain't smart enough to pull off this much crap."

Table had to agree. There was only one other direction this could go.

"Lori."

"Bingo, my brother. Ever since she moved in, shit's been happening. That chick has a past and somethin' ain't right about it. As I see it, you got a few choices. You can kick her ass out and make her leave town. The club will give her a nice escort down the highway to make sure she's gone, and we'll keep our eyes out to make sure she don't come back."

Table bristled and nearly ran off the carefully drawn

lines of the piece he was working on. "Not gonna happen."

Ditch titched his tongue. "I figured that was the case, but I had to point it out. You got feelin's for this woman?"

Table's answer was monosyllabic but full of meaning. He looked up from his work and met Ditch's eye with an unwavering gaze. "Yes."

"Fuck me," Ditch muttered under his breath. "Alrighty then, option two is you hunker down at the farm and see to all your ladies as best you can. That's gonna spread you mighty thin as you can't even keep up now. The club will cover as best we can, but technically, your status is nomad and our chapter is too small to do what you need done. We can help out, but we can't make no promises."

Table resumed his work, a frown of frustration on his face. "Tell me something I don't know."

Ditch took a breath. "Option three. You get your shit together and head back to your own chapter in Bryson City, and not just for a visit. The Lair is a fucking fortress and there are more club brothers there who can watch your back 24/7. You also got more brain power. Bruiser looks like a big dumb lug, but I've heard he's a fucking master computer whiz. I bet my left nut he can dig up whatever info you need to protect your people."

Table finished up the last of the shading on his client's body. The shining face of the kid stared at him from the man's reddened flesh. The man had come to him for a picture of the child he'd lost to leukemia, and Table could relate to the fierceness of that love.

"If I was in your shoes, buddy, I'd pick door number

three," the client said. "You do you, pal, but if it was my kid and my woman, I'd not risk any more than I had to and take as much help as I could get."

Table's mouth thinned as he taped gauze over the new ink. He muttered the aftercare instructions and handed the client a sheet of paper with the same. Ditch left with a finger flick and a *see ya, bro.*

Table took his time cleaning up his area and prepping for the next person. The vandalism had actually been pretty good for business, as it seemed everybody wanted to come get a tattoo from the shop that had its front window busted in. Walk-ins had picked up quite a bit, and Table's chair always seemed to have a body in it, ready to get inked. The next person was a college girl and she wanted the Latin motto of the university scripted on her forearm. *Levos Oculos Meos In Montes*—I lift my eyes to the Mountains. Table was silent as he drew out the phrases directly on the girl's skin. She approved it and he began to work, giving only a half-ear to her wincing and chatter.

Mountains, he thought, his mind whirling and planning. Ditch was right. His club brothers at the Lair were strong and loyal. He had roots there, deep ones. Brick was a tough old man, fair, protective of his people and even more so of the women taken under the club's wing. The chapter here in Asheville was still a good one but small and didn't quite have the same depth of solidarity as his home chapter in Bryson City. Something was threatening his family and he needed to find out what it was and put a stop to it. Ditch was also right in that his ex, Tamara, wasn't smart enough to plan anything out. He hadn't heard squat from her and he wasn't so sure she was even in the picture in the first place. Too many unanswered questions, and too many coincidences were leading him back to the one person who didn't fit in his timeline: Lori. The dyed choppy hair, the insistence on cash only, lack of banking, lack of proper ID, the fear she had shown toward him when she first came to the farm; every sign was pointing to a woman on the run from something bad and that bad something may have found her. Now his family could be in the crosshairs. Table never had been a man to sit on the sidelines and wait for something to happen. He was a man of action, and it was high time for him to take some.

He finished up the elaborate script and the girl squealed a bit as she looked at it. College kids. Table put a smile on his face for her as he took her credit card and swiped it in the machine. Chrissy was working on a back piece and Jack had another college girl in his chair, getting a belly button piercing. No one was in the waiting area for a change, so it was a good time.

"I'm takin' a break for a few minutes. Be outside if you need me," he called out. Jack nodded as he pushed the needle through the girl's clamped skin. She cried out and clenched the hand of her friend.

Table left the building and stood on the street outside watching the people wander in and out of the shops. He lifted his phone, scrolled through his contacts, and hit dial. He raised the phone to his ear and waited for the person at the other end to pick up.

CHAPTER 16

I closed my cheap phone with a snap and nearly collapsed on the kitchen floor of the house Connie and I were cleaning. Papers were finally filed. It was nearly done. No more delays. One more week and I would be free! Tears gathered in my eyes and my throat worked to hold back the sobs of sheer joy I felt.

"*Chingada!* Oh my God, Lori, what's wrong?" Connie's concerned face appeared before mine.

"Nothing," I told her with a big watery smile. "Nothing at all. It's the best it's ever been."

Connie rolled her eyes at me and flipped her hand. "You are one crazy *gringa*! I'm almost finished with the bathrooms. You good in here?"

I sniffed. "Yeah, I'll be done in a minute. Just gotta dump the mop water and put the cleaning stuff up."

"Cool. Anita and I are having a ladies' night tonight. If it's really 'the best it's ever been,' maybe you want to go too?"

"You're not going out with Ditch?"

"Not tonight. A girl has to have some time with her sisters and leave the man at home from time to time. Keeps them on their toes, ya know?"

I was flattered that Connie thought of me as a sister, and yes, I did feel like celebrating. However, the first person I thought of to celebrate with was not my boss. It was Table. He had become the rock in my life, a stable anchor that I needed so badly. At the same time, I felt my heart jolt at the thought that when he found out everything, he would turn his back on me with disgust at what I had done. I could fool myself into thinking he would forgive me, but in my experience, reality never lived up to the dream of it. He wouldn't hurt me physically, but I knew my heart would suffer when he left. I had fallen for the single dad biker and I would never let him know.

"Sure, I'll go. I still don't have a vehicle so I'll have to bum a ride."

Connie giggled. "No problem, *mi hermana*. You can buy the first round!"

We finished up the house, got paid, and left. Connie dropped me off at the farm and told me what time she would be back to get me. I spent some time playing with Angel and hanging with Carol. Martha had gone to Walmart and I knew it would be a long time before she got back. I had been shopping with her before. She loved Walmart and could spend hours at the giant store, poking through the bins of five-dollar DVDs, looking at baby clothes, shoes, grumbling about the cost of kitchenware, and buying piles of groceries for the huge chest freezers in the big storage building. Her favorite joke was to buy any item that said "buy one, get one free." She would hand me one and tell me I owed her as she was taking the freebie.

The weather had warmed up enough in the last two weeks to melt all the ice and snow that had caused my wreck. As the saying went for North Carolina weather, "if you don't like it, just wait a few minutes and it will change." The air was still cold, but without any wind blowing, it didn't feel too bad. The sun was out, and the vivid colors of the mountains were bright and inviting. I stood at the back porch, listening to the sounds of the running creek and trying to identify this new feeling that filled me. It took me a while, but I finally figured it out. I was happy. I hadn't been happy in so long that it was foreign to me. One more week. Seven more days, and the time was counting down.

One thing about happiness was that it was fragile and could break anytime or anywhere. I should have known better. The moment I spotted the silky scarf tied to the rail of the staircase that led to my room, I felt that happiness turn to sheer terror.

No! Not when I'm this close!

My shock was broken by the lubbing sound of Martha's truck returning from her Walmart adventure.

"Dang fool!" she griped as she slammed the door. "I don't know what fire that asshole was after that he almost run me off the road. Damn Jeep was takin' his road half out th' middle and weren't gonna move none. I had to take the shoulder so that dumbass didn't sideswipe me when he passed. Damn idjit!"

I tore my eyes away from the scarf and moved in a trance to help Martha unload the mound of plastic bags in the bed.

"Got me some of them squeezie panties. Supposed to make you look thin an' keep all your jiggly parts still. Shoulda picked up some for Carol. You okay?"

It took me a moment to realize Martha was talking to me instead of rambling. "Yes, I'm fine."

She snorted. "You don't look fine. You're white as a sheet and look like you're 'bout to keel over. Maybe you need t' sit for a spell."

Table's bike roared down the driveway. Anytime the weather allowed it, he would ride rather than drive. After riding with him, I understood the preference. He parked and stalked over to us, his face dark and serious.

"Get them bags out th' back and in the house. Imma gonna check on Carol and show her my new underduds. Might get me one a' them push-up bras I seen on the shoppin' channel."

Table's tight face went slack at Martha's words. He shook his head. "Jesus, Nanny! You need to learn when to filter."

She laughed and shuffled under the weight of several bags. I picked up a few more in each hand and Table grabbed the rest. His presence was comforting even though he looked like he could chew up and spit nails.

"We need to talk." His words sounded like crunching gravel.

I nodded and glanced once more at the fluttering scarf.

We finished hauling the bags into the kitchen, and I listened as Carol fussed about all the extra stuff that had not been on the shopping list. Martha just harrumphed and stuffed the cabinets and pantry with my help. Table checked on his sleeping daughter.

When there was nothing left for me to do, I walked out of the house, my feet leaden with dread. I knew I had to face this, but I really didn't want to. The closer I got to the scarf, the more panic I felt crawl in my throat. The fabric was a finely spun blend of pale gold threads that shimmered in the early evening light. I had always loved the way it felt around my neck—until the night I learned to hate it. That was the last time I'd seen this scarf.

Tears clogged my eyes and I rushed up the steps, nearly stumbling in my haste. I left that filthy memory tied to the rail and I hoped like hell that maybe it would stay there and rot. I yanked out my duffle and began randomly stuffing my clothes in it. My cash stash was in a separate bag and I grabbed it, dumping the contents on the bed. The pile of money looked like a lot, but for life on the run it was a pitiful amount. Nevertheless, I owed Table for my van and I wasn't stupid enough to think it was a cheap fix. I raked out about half of the cash and jammed the rest back into the money bag.

"What the fuck?"

I jerked back with a cry and braced myself against the bed. My heart was pounding and I could feel my body jerking with every beat. Blood roared in my ears and I suddenly couldn't draw enough breath.

"Shit, Lori, sit down before you fall down."

Table approached me and the wild panic suddenly disappeared. My knees couldn't hold me up anymore. He lunged and caught me as I buckled.

"Fuck, baby girl," he said into my hair.

He was warm. Solid. My anchor. I grabbed his jacket and burrowed into him, clinging with everything I had in me. Violent shivers racked my body as the adrenaline spike hit its peak and I gasped for air, my face pressed against his chest. He smelled of spicy leather, baby powder, and man. His arms came around me and he crooned soothing words while he held tight.

I didn't know how long we stood there before the shaking subsided and the tears dried up. I pushed against the cocoon of Table's body and freed myself.

"I'm okay now." My heart was still pounding, but my voice was steady, if a bit rough.

"No, you're not" was his firm return. "I don't think you've been okay for a long time, but you're gonna be."

Fresh tears threatened. He gestured to the piles of money on the bed.

"What the hell is this?"

I sniffed. "I was leaving you half of what I have to help pay you for at least some of the work Ditch did on my van. I'll send more when I can."

Table shook his head. "There's a problem with that, baby girl. You ain't leavin'."

My swollen eyes blinked. "I have to, Table. It's for your own protection."

His face showed a mixture of humor and exasperation. "You just don't get it, do you, Lori?" He pointed to the patch on his cut. "Do you know what this emblem means? I told you once already, but I see it didn't stick. I'm a Dragon Runner, baby girl. We would give up our lives for those under the protection of our wings, and I have a huge army of brothers ready to be at my back anytime I call, just as I'm ready to be at their backs when I'm called. Everyone at this farm is under those wings, and that includes you. In case you haven't figured it out, you belong to me. You are mine. The club may look like a freewheeling party crowd, but I promise you, there is not another group you'll ever find in this lifetime that is more loyal or devoted than the Dragon Runners."

I decided to ignore the possessive words for now and shook my head. "You don't understand. He's rich and his family has a lot of power."

I sucked in a breath at what I'd just revealed. It didn't seem to bother Table.

"Rich men bleed just the same as poor ones. How 'bout we sit down for a bit and you tell me what's going on."

I gave up. Table was patient but relentless. We sat on the bed, disrupting the money. Both of us ignored it.

"You're going to hate me," I said. I was surprised how steady I sounded. "You're going to hate me for bringing this danger to your family."

"Hate is a strong word, baby girl. I can't tell you I won't get mad, but I can tell you I'll hear you out and I will not let loose. You already know I will never raise a hand against you no matter what. I told you I had your back and I meant it."

He placed a finger under my chin and tipped my head back. The sincerity in his face was almost unbearable. "You're a smart woman, Lori. You know there's something between us and it's good. Real good. So good I'm willing to fight for it, and that includes fightin' you to keep it. We've been going slow, but I think it's time we put our cards down. I just laid claim to you and that's all of you, includin' the bad stuff, and I gotta know what's comin' our way. Can you do that for me, baby girl? Can you find it in your heart to trust me?"

My heart was pounding out of my chest. Was it time? Should I take this chance? My head churned with agonizing thoughts, but it had come to sink or swim. Table was the best man I'd ever known and if I was ever going to get my life back, I had to start somewhere. I took a deep breath and dove off the cliff.

"My name is not Lori Mathews. It's Vivian Townsend. The same Vivian you've heard about on the news that is supposed to be in South Africa working to build schools for the Townsend Foundation. The same Vivian that is still married to Jeffrey Townsend Jr., son of Senator Townsend."

Table didn't move or speak. He just looked at me steadily, waiting until I opened up and told him my story. I closed my eyes, took another deep, ragged breath, and lanced that festering wound.

CHAPTER 17

I heard the front door slam and he yelled at his bodyguard to get the fuck out. My stomach clenched and fingers of cold dread drifted across my neck. He was upset over something. It was not good when he was upset.

I was sitting in my robe, in front of my vanity, making my preparations for the evening's event and had tied my favorite gold scarf around my neck instead of wearing one of the ornate necklaces I owned. We were supposed to go to a fundraiser at one of the art galleries in a couple of hours, and I prayed that having a public appearance would keep him under control this time. I ran a brush through my long blonde hair and pretended to preen even as I heard him coming up the stairs.

"Vivian!" His yell was harsh. I flinched and cleared my throat.

"I'm in the bedroom." My light voice didn't reflect the fear in my gut. I saw his reflection in the vanity mirror. His face was calm and tight. This was bad. If he were yelling

and screaming at me, it would be better. He would get all his anger out, and even if I was bleeding from his words, I wouldn't be bleeding anywhere else. I glanced at the clock.

"I'll be ready to go soon if you want to get to the gallery earlier than you originally planned." I swiped on some mascara and willed my hand to stay steady. He came up behind me and stroked a hand over my hair, and lightly pulled at the scarf.

"Vivian, what did you do today?"

My mind raced through the day's activities, trying to pinpoint what it was that I'd done wrong.

"I got the housework and dinner schedule set up for next week. I took care of replying to the charity invitation you wanted to attend, and I got tickets to the opera, but I couldn't get the box seats you wanted. Senator Bishop already had them, but I know you're trying to win his favor so I thought you'd be okay with it. I—"

"Shut up."

My mouth snapped closed as his grip tightened on my hair.

"The spa, Vivian. You went to the fucking spa."

I had gone to the spa. Before these big meet-and-greet dinner fundraisers, he wanted me to look as pristine and perfect as I could. The spa meant waxing, polishing, facial, hair, nails, eyebrows, the works. Occasionally I got a massage to help me relax and hopefully get through whatever event I had to attend. I dropped the mascara wand. I had gotten a massage today. My regular person was out sick and the spa only had one other massage therapist there *at the time.*

"You let a man touch you today. Mimi Carson was at the spa and saw it."

I swallowed. Sherman was a small, thin man and one of the sweetest people at the spa. He was also very gay and very open about being gay. He had come bouncing into the room announcing himself with a drawn-out "Helloooooooo, precious!" He wasn't a quiet person as he pounded and worked on my shoulders and back, spending the forty-five-minute session talking about the latest crisis in his life with his boyfriend and his boyfriend's cat. I was thoroughly entertained by his attitude and detailed drama.

"Marianna was out and Sherman—"

"A fuckin' black man!"

That was it. Pain bit into my throat as he jerked me from the vanity stool using the scarf and threw me to the floor. I didn't have time to curl into a ball before his foot landed in my belly. Air whooshed from my lungs and I gasped for any air I could get. He grabbed the scarf again and yanked me up, drawing the cloth tight and choking me. He smashed a fist in my face, knocking me back to the floor. I felt my lip split and my mouth fill with blood as I gasped for air.

"Goddamn slut! How long have you been cheating on me?"

"I haven't. Sherman is gay." My words were garbled by my swelling mouth, but it didn't matter what I said. I'd already been judged... again.

"Liar!" He kicked me again in the back and I held back from crying out. I'd learned that making any pained

noises only made it worse. As the beating continued, he yelled over and over again, calling me names, calling out every imagined slight or wrong I had done. I begged. I apologized. I prayed someone in the house would hear and care enough to come help me. I felt something in my ribs give when he gave me one particularly vicious kick. This time I did scream. My arm broke when he stomped on it as I was trying to crawl away. My nose broke as well when he slammed my face into the floor.

He didn't stop there. What he did next was far worse than I'd ever thought he would do. He jerked me onto my back, and I screamed again in agony. He tore open my robe and forced my legs apart. I didn't know which pain was worse: the one of him ripping into my body or the one in my brain of not being able to stop him.

When he was done, he got off me. He pulled his pants up and ran his hands over his hair to put it in some sense of order. His rage was burned out and he winced as he looked down on me, maybe realizing he'd gone too far this time.

"I'll tell the hosts you were feeling unwell and decided not to come. There's a virus going around, so that's plausible."

He went into the bathroom and I heard the shower come on. The action of closing my legs was agonizing, and I knew there was blood. A lot of it. I lay there in one big ball of pain until I heard the shower go off. I spurred myself to move, rolling over to my good side and pushing myself up with one arm. My ribs throbbed and I couldn't take a breath without pain stabbing me. I managed to pull myself up and right the fallen vanity stool as he came through the bedroom and headed into the closet. The scent of his spicy aftershave followed him. At one time, I'd loved smelling the masculine cologne. Now it made me want to gag. I sat on the low stool and leaned on my vanity, trying to breathe steadily. My arm was useless, my lip was hurting and still bleeding, and there was a burning between my legs that topped it all. I lifted my blackening eyes to the mirror and saw his reflection as he emerged from the closet, dressed in his tuxedo and tails. He was a devastatingly handsome man, but all I could see was the monster inside.

My throat was raw and I swallowed the copper-tasting saliva that gathered in my mouth. "I need a hospital." My mouth wasn't working right so my words came out garbled.

He came over and stood behind me, his fingers working the black bow tie at his neck. "Not tonight. It wouldn't look right. I'll have Bobby run your car into a tree or something tomorrow afternoon. I'm busy in the morning. We'll time it for after lunch so I can be with you in the emergency room. It will make a pretty good photo op with me at the side of my lovely wife after she carelessly wrecked. You'll need to clean this mess up before tomorrow morning. I'll stay somewhere else tonight, and that will give you plenty of time to get yourself together."

He leaned over and pressed his lips to my head, and it took everything I had left not to flinch away and set him off again.

I didn't move until I heard the front door close after he left. The silence was heavy. There was no other movement or sound in the house. If any workers were left, they would stay out of the way and avoid this part of the house for fear of seeing something they didn't want to get involved in. I was alone and no one would stop me.

There was still light outside, and people in the affluent neighborhood would be walking their dogs, or jogging, or strolling along the neatly kept sidewalks. I had time, but I was fading fast. I forced myself upright and staggered to the bedroom door. Just that bit of effort had me seeing black spots in front of my eyes. I heard a noise in the upper hallway, but it was footsteps quickly moving away. I didn't bother to call for help, as I knew I wouldn't get it. Somehow I got down the staircase without falling. Each step jarred my ribs and I could barely move my legs in more than a shuffle.

I made it halfway down the drive before my legs gave out. I dropped to my knees, adding more scrapes and bruises to my collection. I did the only thing I could do.

I crawled.

The asphalt was rough and took more skin from my one good hand and knees, but that pain simply blended into all the rest. The scarf fell away from my neck and I left it there. I briefly thought about the security cameras and if someone was in the house monitoring them, watching my slow progress and calling my husband to come deal with his errant wife. I was close. I got to the gates and stared up at the control that would open them, wondering how I was going to pull myself up to get to it. Apparently, someone was watching from inside the house and decided to be merciful. I heard the click and they swung open. I halfway expected my husband to come through, but all I heard was chirping birds and the hum of automatic sprinklers coming on.

I crawled onward, dragging my broken arm, my body in agonizing pain. I finally collapsed into the fragrant grass of the wide median strip between the sidewalk and the street. It was cool and smelled so clean. My eyes were nearly swollen shut, but I saw the clover. It was right in front of my face, four bright green leaves attached to a thin stem. It shone at me like a beacon. I reached out my good hand and stroked the round discs, hoping this was a sign that my luck was about to change. I noticed the pristine white of the sidewalk and the cerulean blue of the early evening sky. A strange sense of peace came over me as I stared at the tiny plant. Blackness was swirling in front of my eyes and I was fading fast. If I was going to die here on the sidewalk, at least I would die free.

I heard a voice shouting, "Oh my God!" and then sirens in the distance.

I might have laughed if I'd had the breath to do so. I knew the sirens were for me and whoever opened the gates had had enough integrity to call emergency services. I stroked the clover over and over again, hoping to glean more of its luck. The sirens got louder and pulled up next to me, and I heard the slam of doors and rattle of other equipment being gathered. I took one last look at my clover, still standing tall, and let the blackness take me.

* * *

Tears rolled from my eyes as I finished the rest of my story.

"I was sent to a private clinic in a small town in northern West Virginia, along with two bodyguards to 'keep me safe.' I think it was more to keep me isolated and under control. The doctors fixed me up, and I stayed there until I healed. My father-in-law came to visit me once. I can still remember him standing over me, lecturing me on what was going to happen next. He'd spent a huge amount of money to keep the news of the 'incident' out of the papers and to purge the police and hospital records.

"Jeffrey Jr. had been sent to South America and he concocted the story for the press that Jeff and I were on a humanitarian mission for the foundation and would be out of the country for a while. After I was back on my feet, I was expected to return to Washington and continue my role in the foundation and Jeff's career. I think he had visions of Jeff becoming the next Senator Townsend, and being charged with domestic violence and rape wouldn't go over well with voters. He said divorce was not an option. His instructions were I was to stay married to Jeff, smile, and play my part like a good little wife. Obviously, I disagreed. A few days before I was supposed to be discharged, I came back to my room after breakfast and found a flash drive, pictures of my injuries in a big envelope, copies of the police's reports, and five hundred dollars. There was a set of car keys too. I'm guessing one of the guards did it, but I really don't know. What I did know was I couldn't stomach the idea of going back to that life. I didn't know what else to do so I took everything and ran."

Table grunted behind me and his arms tightened again.

"What was on the flash drive? I'm guessin' you took a look at it?"

"Yes, I did. I opened it only once at an online café. I expected to see digital copies of the papers I had in hand, but it was about the foundation's finances. Lists of account numbers to projects I'd never heard of and rivers of money running through them. I think I was looking at a massive money laundering scam or maybe tax fraud, but I don't know for sure. All I know is, what I had was powerful and dangerous." I swallowed the lump in my throat. There was a lot to unpack and once I started, it kept running like a broken faucet. With each sentence, freedom filled me and the sense of impending dread I'd carried with me for the last year lightened.

"I'm not rich like Jeff's family, but I do have a small trust fund my parents left me that he can't get to. I can't get to it now either. If I tried to access that money, the Senator or Jeffrey might be able to have it traced. I was scared what they would be capable of if they found me. Maybe I've seen too many spy movies, but I didn't want to take any chances of leaving a paper trail. I sold the car and started working under the table jobs for cash only. As far as my marriage was concerned, it was over, but I still wanted to get an official divorce. I needed it for my own peace. My dad's attorney has been with my family for years and he's been the only person I could trust up until now. All our communication has been through burner phones, and I sent him copies of everything but the flash drive. He was only to use the pictures and reports, letting the Senator know I only wanted a quiet divorce from Jeffrey and that was all.

"I was afraid if my lawyer had a copy of the flash drive that would put him and his family in danger. Essentially, I was blackmailing the Senator for my divorce. He didn't like it and still doesn't, but it's happening. I can't imagine the money he's spent to keep it out of the news. I'm sure that if he found me, somehow he'd find a way to make me go back or kill me. If he knew I had this flash drive, I'd be dead already. He may suspect it anyway. This is another reason I've gone as far off the grid as possible and done whatever I could to stay that way. It's taken so many months for the divorce to happen. Delays, protests from the senator, signatures and arguments that took forever due to Jeff being out of the country, but finally it's happening. My lawyer is getting the final divorce papers next week. He has proxy to sign and I'll be free or at least I hope I'm free."

Table stayed silent the entire time I spoke. The only indication he was listening was when his arm tightened around my middle and he made a sharp inhale. Sometime during my recounting, he maneuvered us so we were laying on the bed, on our sides with him against my back. His heavy arms encircled me, and he was snugged up tight, his legs crooked and molded to mine. The enveloping security I felt was overwhelming.

"Table?"

"Gimme a minute, Lori." He growled the words, as if he held rocks in his mouth. I didn't know if this was good or bad. I could feel his breath against the back of my neck and tingles ran down my spine from the warmth. I sniffed, determined to hold back more tears that threatened to fall.

"I'm not sure, but I think someone has been chasing me. That stuff that's been happening around the farm? I think maybe Jeff or the senator paid someone to harass me and make me run again. It's happened a few times before. I was in Canton, working as a dishwasher in a diner that was broken into one night, like the tattoo parlor. I left before the police and press could find and question me. I swept floors and was cleaning for cash at a bar in Bluefield when someone keyed a bunch of cars in the parking lot. The ones that were damaged were all around my car, but it was the only one that was untouched. I left from there and kept moving, never staying in one place for more than a few weeks until I came here. No one has ever been hurt before, but the incident with the van came very close. I think because the divorce is all but official, he's getting worse. I still may just be paranoid. Maybe once the papers are filed, I can disappear, and he'll stop bothering me."

Table's breath tickled my ear. "Then what? You can't go back to bein' Vivian Townsend again. And the news about the divorce is bound to come out sooner or later."

"Maybe they would spin the story as me being unfaithful and Jeffrey divorced me instead of the other way around. I didn't really think that far ahead. I just wanted to get away and get my life back." I stopped trying to check them and let the tears flow freely down my face and puddle under my cheeks. "I'm so sorry I brought this trouble to you and your family. I'll leave first thing in the morning."

"No, you won't." Table shifted restlessly. "I suspect you

may be right. Someone is definitely fuckin' with my family, but you're in my family. They fuck with one, they fuck with all of us. My family protects its own." His voice was low and heavy. He squeezed me again.

"I don't mean to sound negative, Table, but you have two old women and a baby here."

He sighed against my neck and the tiny hairs all along my spine pricked up in a thrilling, sensitive wave. "You still don't quite get it, Lori. When I say my family, I'm talking about the biggest badass brotherhood ever known in the history of these mountains. There's not one club brother who won't throw down for me when I call, no questions asked. The Dragon Runners live in peace with the rest of the world, and we like it like that. The club works hard to keep it that way, but anyone starts somethin' with us, we've been known to finish it. Whoever is doing this shit brought it to the wrong house. Yeah, you're leavin', but you ain't leavin' tomorrow and you ain't goin' alone. Time for me to go home. The Dragon is awake and ready to hunt."

CHAPTER 18

It was nearly a week later, coming up on Valentine's Day, when a light snow fell during the night and coated the trees in a sparkling white blanket. More snow was on the way, but that didn't make Table change his mind about traveling. The drive wasn't a long one, but it felt like we went to another country. Most of the drive was on highways so we didn't have any problems in Table's truck. By we, I meant Table, Angel, and me. Martha and Carol both insisted they stay at their own place. Martha's exact words were "no damn Yankee's gonna make me move!" Ditch and several others from the Asheville Dragon Runners chapter volunteered to stay there at the farm at night. Even better, one of the other grandsons was planning on moving into the room I'd just vacated. I could tell that brought Table some relief. He had finished all of his lingering clients at Asheville Ink. I had helped Connie with a few more clients, and Maddie from the bar had taken over for the rest. We were free and clear.

Angel was as good as gold on the trip, sleeping most

of the way and cooing the few moments she was awake. I, on the other hand, had been suffering from insomnia and worry for the last week, ever since finding that damned scarf. Nothing else had happened, but still every creak and noise at night had me spooked. Table insisted I move into the main house, but in deference to Carol's views, Table slept on the couch and I took his bed.

We arrived at the Lair late in the morning and were greeted by an enthusiastic Betsey, who immediately claimed Angel. I felt like I was being welcomed back home, and the tension of the last few weeks melted from me, leaving exhaustion in its wake.

"Brick and the other Runners are waiting on me, baby girl. We got church called the moment we got here. Get on back to my room for a bit and get some rest."

"Church?"

"Yeah. It's what we call a meeting of the club members. It shouldn't take too long but still, you need to grab some shut-eye while you can."

My eyes were growing heavier as he walked me back to his room. Sleep seemed like a great idea.

"What about Angel?"

Table's light chuckle hit my ears. "Don't worry about Angel. You've already seen how Betsey loves to be grandma to everyone. No tellin' how spoiled she's gonna get."

He pressed his lips one last time to my forehead. "Now quit fightin' it and rest. I'll come check on you later."

I heard the door click shut and then I was out like a light.

* * *

Table entered the meeting room to a round of one-armed man hugs and back slaps. Everyone was glad to see him back in the fold and not shy about showing it. Table felt humbled by the attention and relieved by it as well. When he had driven up to the Lair earlier, he'd had the sense of being the prodigal son returning home at last. This place was where he belonged.

"All right, people, we got some stuff to talk about." Brick sat down heavily in the padded chair at the end of a long table, custom carved with the symbol of the Dragon Runners MC. "Table's already spoke to me 'bout some stuff, but there's more we need to know. Table, the floor is yours. What's going on?"

Table took a big breath and outlined the last months. The problems at the farm, the deliberate tampering with her van, the vandalism, Tamara's sudden change of heart about Angel, and Lori's story of being Vivian Townsend and why she was hiding. When he spoke about the attack and the rape, audible growls were heard in the room and the temperature dropped to ice cold.

"Half the news lately has been about the foundation being investigated. Seems like someone else has blown the whistle on their accounting mess. The Senator has claimed his son and daughter-in-law gave him control by proxy, but there's not been proof of that and the numbers don't add up." Stud speculated while tapping his fingers on the smooth wood surface. "He's got plenty of legal troubles that put him in a big steaming pile of shit, and there's videos out there that Jeffery is whooping it up somewhere other than where he's supposed to be. According to the press, the FBI is asking a lot of questions the good senator can't answer, some of those being about Vivian. Or Lori, as she calls herself now. She makes a sudden appearance, she may be in as much legal trouble as the rest of them. That flash drive is her only ticket out."

Dodge cracked his knuckles. "Seems to me Mr. Townsend needs to produce his daughter-in-law posthaste. Doesn't make a lotta sense to chase her down or harass her. Why try to kill her with the brake thing on the van?"

Mute, who'd lost his voice due to a vicious fight when he was younger, typed a single word in his phone and turned it to Brick to read aloud.

"Money."

Table shook his head. "Lori mentioned that she has a trust fund she turned over to her lawyer for safekeeping. She said he can't get to it and she can't either until after the divorce is final. I have no idea how much money she has in the trust, but she said it's peanuts compared to what the senator has."

Brick steepled his fingers under his beard. "Ain't her money they're after. It's the foundation money and from what you're sayin', I 'spect she don't got a clue 'bout what them assholes is doin' to it. Dirty Senator. Asshole wife-beater ex. Fuckin' FBI. That's a lot of baggage for a woman to carry. I don't know this Lori or Vivian or whatever the hell her name is. Betsey said she's good for your Angel and is a sweet girl. Right now that's all she is. A sweet girl. She ain't an old lady and not even claimed by the club.

That gonna change soon, Table?"

Table knew what Brick was asking. "Yup. I claim her, and sometime in the future she's gonna be my old lady. We ain't there yet and I don't need to tell you why she's hanging back, but it will happen."

"You love this woman?"

Table looked at his club president dead in the eye. "I'd take a bullet for her."

Brick nodded in affirmation. "All right then. Bruiser, take the flash drive and get on that computer of yours. Dig around for whatever shit is out there on these two Townsend assholes. We don't know what's coming, so everyone rides with protection and no one rides alone. I ain't gonna lock down the Lair unless we get a real threat, though. Them fellas ain't got much in the way of balls if they think puttin' out scarves 'n' breakin' windows is gonna scare us."

Table waved at the large man sporting a short bobbed ponytail on the back of his balding head. "Hey, Bruiser, mind doin' a check on the court mess Tamara is throwing at me?"

"Sure thing, brother. It'll cost you though. I want a tattoo of a sugar skull on my left shoulder."

Table grinned and stuck out his hand. Bruiser grasped it and pumped twice.

Dodge leaned back. "We 'bout done here? There's a beer and a shot in the big room with my name on it, just waitin' for me."

Brick tapped his gavel on the table once. "Adjourned. Now let's get some grub and booze. My beautiful Betsey is ready to get this party started so we can welcome our brother home good an' proper."

CHAPTER 19

I woke up groggy but feeling better than I had in a long time. I didn't know if it was the purest of mountain air or the sense of security I felt that had caused me to sleep so hard. I got up and rummaged through my stuff to find fresh clothes. The shower was hot and I wished I could stay under the spray a bit longer. My hair was growing out, showing golden blonde roots, and soon I'd have to make a decision about what to do with it. The short black-dyed do was not my favorite, but it had served its purpose in keeping me hidden.

I had just finished putting on jeans, a tank top, and a plaid work shirt when I heard a knock at the door. Table opened it and stuck his head inside. "You hungry? Betsey's got chili on the stove and homemade cornbread."

My stomach gurgled at the thought of food. "Yeah, I am. Where's Angel?"

"On Betsey's hip. I'm never gonna get my daughter back."

His look was so exaggerated, I laughed lightly.

He came over to me without asking and folded me into his strong arms. "It's gonna be fine, baby girl."

I had come to love the endearment that at one time I'd hated.

He cupped my cheek and raised my head to look into my eyes. "I need to know something before we go out and join the crowd. Vivian or Lori?"

I looked up into his gaze and only saw gentleness. "I don't know," I answered honestly.

He nodded. "I figured it was confusing to you as well. I'm still gonna call you Lori. That's how I met you and that's how I know you. This Vivian person's not real to me."

I thought for a moment. "You know, even when I was Vivian, I don't think I was a real person. I've been Lori for only a year and have been more real as her than I ever was as Vivian."

"Where did you get the name?"

"My grandmother's name was Lorelei. She died when I was a child, but I remember her holding me on her lap and singing to me. She loved bright colors and always smelled like flowers. She was the happiest person I knew, and I guess I wanted that for me. Lorelei is a name that stands out a bit, so I shortened it to Lori. Easier to hide."

He lowered his head and brushed my lips with his. I felt that simple touch deep in my belly.

"Your days of hidin' are done. Come on, let's get some food."

The Lair was full of life and sound. Music was playing

and people were laughing, talking, eating, and drinking. Some men wearing their leather cuts were shooting pool and others were playing video games on one of several flat-screen TVs. The club children were running through the adults like an obstacle course, but no one minded except a random shout of "be careful." I had been to many high-society events where the formality was stiff and no one dared act out. I watched Betsey, with Angel on her hip, and the other ladies of the club joke and laugh loud and free. Vivian wouldn't fit in here, but Lori could and she wanted to, badly.

Betsey spotted me and I was whisked through a volley of introductions. I saw Mute and Kat. Mute was a little frightening, but his frown softened every time he looked at his wife, Katrina. Stud and Eva looked like complete opposites, but anyone with eyes in their head could tell he was totally devoted to her. She was starting to show her pregnancy and it was funny to watch him fuss over her and her fuss right back at him for hovering. Table took my hand and held it the entire time, not leaving my side once. I noticed I wasn't just introduced as Lori. I was Lori, Table's girl. I would never be able to describe in a million years how good that felt.

I watched Tambre and Molly refresh the food table with new pots of chili. The spicy aroma set my mouth watering and my stomach gurgling again.

"Food?"

Table's single-syllable question was all I needed. We moved to the table, and the club president approached us. I had seen

Brick earlier but had not been formally introduced. He was someone I'd heard enough about that I was a bit scared of him. He was stout with gray-streaked auburn hair and beard, and there was an aura of power around him. His smile to me was nice, but his eyes were steely. I couldn't tell if he was friend or foe, and I shrank into Table's body like a turtle. Brick must have picked up on the movement, because he shared a look with Table that seemed confirming.

"Nice to meetcha, Lori. Name's Brick. I 'spect you know who I am."

"Yes, I do. Nice to meet you too, Mr. Brick."

His expression lightened up and he fought back a grin. "Ain't no mister, darlin'. Just Brick. Papa to my own grandkids and everyone else's here. I know Betsey has a few other names for me, but none Imma gonna say in public."

I chuckled lightly while Table let out a huge belly laugh. "You ain't lyin'! I've heard Betsey get her dander up at you more than once."

Brick huffed. "Love that woman from the bottom of my heart and I wouldn't trade her for the world, but there are times I think about it."

Table laughed again. "Damn, Brick. Your mouth's gonna get you in trouble."

"Wouldn't be the first time."

He stuck his hand out to me. "I know you've got a lot of bad going on. I'm here to let you know the Dragon Runners got your back."

I looked at his giant outstretched paw and place my hand in it. He pumped it twice and let go. That was it. I knew from conversations with Table that Brick was old-school and a handshake from him was a binding contract. This was a humbling experience and I had the urge to cry. "Thank you."

Betsey came up with a serious look on her face and a sleepy Angel nestled on her shoulder. "Imma put the baby down for the night. You need to come see what just came on the news."

Several people had gathered around the giant screen. "Breaking news" scrolled across the bottom while live camera footage rolled with a split screen of a newsroom and a reporter desperately trying to keep up with a crowd.

"We come to you live from the capital where this evening, Senator Jeffrey Townsend has been formally charged with embezzlement and fraud in connection with the Townsend Foundation. He has been placed under arrest pending an arraignment in the next few days."

The TV screen showed a shaky clip of my father-in-law being led out of his house in handcuffs. I used to think he was the ultimate power in Washington. Now he just looked like an old man. The film clip ended and an image of my ex and me in formal attire came up. I remembered when that picture was taken. Jeff was in his tuxedo, smiling and dashing, making it appear we were the perfect couple. I was in an iridescent cream-colored gown, my long golden hair pulled back in a classic chignon, and a diamond choker sparkling at my neck. I had my gold scarf around my shoulders to hide the latest round of bruises. I smiled brightly, but my eyes were empty.

"Senator Townsend and his family foundation has been under FBI investigations for months, triggered by an anonymous source within the Townsend's personal staff. Both Jeff Jr. and Vivian Townsend were reported to have left the country for a philanthropic and humanitarian mission; however, up until now, no one has heard from them except through foundation emails."

The image cut to the long-distance one that had been making the rounds on Facebook and Twitter.

"Photographs have surfaced showing Jeff Townsend with a Brazilian model and have been confirmed as being legitimate. Vivian Townsend has not been seen or heard from since their supposed mission trip. Rumors have been circulating for months that foul play has occurred and Vivian Townsend is deceased. We'll bring you details as they become available. This is Martin Ford with WK—"

The screen went as blank as my face. I could feel eyes on me as I stared at the dark TV. The room was deathly quiet and I started shaking. Tears formed in my eyes and I fought to keep them from tracking down my face. I lost.

"I'm—I'm sorry, I don't know—I—"

"Hush, baby girl, I got you. No one here's judging. You're in the family now," Table muttered, pressing my face into his chest.

"Damn straight." The declaration had me looking up. Betsey had come back from putting the baby down and was heading our way. "Problem with some folks is they get so fancy that they forget that we commoners have more going on than they think. This club is a strong one and a smart one.

Ain't nothing gonna break the line of this brotherhood. You can take that to the bank, cash it, and spend it."

Betsey hugged me and I suddenly found myself surrounded by Dragon Runners and their women. Mute looked like he was ready to chew nails and smile while doing it. I wasn't sure who looked more determined, Stud or Eva. Brick cleared his throat.

"I been around a long time. I seen a lotta stuff 'n' met a lotta different people. Black, white, brown, don't matter none to me. I seen rich people with so much money they don't know what to do with it and I been around some poorer than a church mouse. Fact of the matter is I don't give a rat's ass about money, race, religion, politics, or any of that other shit people get so caught up in they cain't tell their ass from a hole in the ground. All that Facebook postin' crap don't mean nothin'. This club is for riding free and living high and I've spent my whole life makin' and keepin' it that way. There ain't a whole lot I cain't see myself gettin' mad at enough to wake the Dragon, but I can name a few. One is beating up children. Ain't no call for that. Ever. Two is beating up on a woman. Don't matter if she's being a bitch or a pain in the ass, no real man should ever lift his hand against a woman. It ain't right and ain't never gonna be right. A real man don't touch his woman like that. He don't talk her down or call her names. He don't disrespect her and he especially don't hit her. Any man does that shit, ain't no man. He's a fuckin' coward who ain't got the balls to step up. Third is threatenin' my family. Y'all know what that means."

I saw Table and the surrounding Runners nod.

Stud said it out loud. "The Dragon is awake and hunting."

CHAPTER 20

The party didn't continue long after the newsflash. Betsey was the ultimate mother hen, fussing over everyone, issuing orders for the prospects to keep the trash and beer bottles cleared, and then going upstairs to "check on the baby." Kat had been manning the small bar and mixing margaritas. I'd had two of the potent drinks already and was feeling pleasantly buzzed. Table stayed with me, some part of him in constant contact, his arm around me and his finger stroking my shoulder underneath the soft flannel of my shirt, or holding my hand and leaning in to kiss my hair or forehead.

I can't wait to see this grow out. Love to see you wearing your natural blonde color." His eyes took in the black mess on my head.

"You like it better long or short?"

"Don't matter none, as long as it's you wearin' it."

My heart melted. "Table, you have to be the most perfect man I've ever met."

He smiled, and I admired again the brilliant white of his teeth. "Don't set the bar too high, baby girl. I can be a stubborn ass just like the rest. I like my T-shirts folded a certain way and my socks matched up and rolled at the cuffs. My bike is like my second child, and I'm the only one who gets to ride her. I'm sure you got little quirks about you too. That's all little stuff and we'll be learning our way around it. I'm sure there's gonna be times I'll piss you off or you'll piss me off. When that happens, I hope you can remember you're always safe. You can cuss the fire outta me and I won't raise my hand to you. If I lose my shit, I won't take it out on you. I've said all this before, and I'll say it again and again until you believe it."

The warmth in my chest had little to do with the alcohol.

When most of the people (including Betsey) had either left for their homes or drifted to their rooms, Table and I finally called it a night. We went upstairs briefly to check on Angel. All the excitement and attention had exhausted the baby and she was curled in her favorite position, dead to the world asleep. We then made our way back down to the cavernous great room and went down the back hallway to Table's room. I picked up my phone that I had left on the nightstand earlier. I opened it up and found a new text message sent earlier today from my lawyer's New Jersey number. Only two words, but they meant the world.

It's done.

There's a before and after in regards to every life event. The restrictions and waiting before getting a driver's license and then the freedoms in the after. The coming of age when finally turning twenty-one and officially becoming an adult who can go to a bar and drink. The years a couple has together before turning into parents. There was no big party for me after. No fireworks. No shifting of the earth and stars. Just those two words that had my heart full and racing. For so long, I'd felt like I was dragging heavy iron chains covered in padlocks everywhere I went. Two words dropped that weight like it never existed. I was almost giddy.

"You okay, baby girl?"

I looked up into Table's face, at his brow wrinkled in concern. I turned the phone to show him the text.

"The divorce. It's over. I don't know how it's been kept out of the news and I'm not sure I care. I'm free."

His eyes burned into mine as his hand came up to cup my cheek. "That's great, baby girl. Happy for you."

If anyone asked me why I did it, I couldn't say. All I knew was a flash fire ignited in me and I let it take control. I dropped my phone, not caring if it broke, and with both hands I seized Table's shoulder, pulled him down to me, and crushed his mouth to mine. He let me kiss him hard and opened up when I pushed my tongue against his lips. I was burning up with want and my shirt had become stifling. I tore my mouth away from his long enough to yank the flannel from my arms and whip the tank over my head. Then I was back, jerking at his cut and the thermal under it.

Table seemed to know this was a crucial moment. His heat surrounded me and I could sense his desire, his cock hardening against my stomach, but I didn't feel overpowered. I was aware of his presence and his strength but not in a fearful way. He gave me support and patience.

"If you're not ready for this, we don't have to do anything. I'll just hold you in my arms all night if that's what you need."

I wanted to cry at his gruff words. "What I need is to feel you inside me." My voice was husky with a craving I hadn't thought I was capable of.

He hesitated, his fingers stroking over my cheek. Then he shrugged off his cut and reached over his head to the back of his neck, pulling off his shirt in one motion. The bright colors of his tattoos were muted in the dim light but the definition of his muscles was clear. He watched me as he backed toward the bed and slowly lowered his zipper. He wore nothing underneath, and the moment he pulled off his jeans, his hard cock sprang free. Table was not a small man in any sense of the word. He was hefty and thick, and my mouth watered with the need to taste him. He opened a drawer in the nightstand and pulled out a condom packet before getting on the bed. He lay on his back, one hand over his head grabbing the headboard and one hand stroking himself. His eyes stayed on me, his fingers moving slowly over his flesh, waiting for me.

I knew he would wait all night if that's what I needed.

I slipped off my bra. The air was cool against my skin and goose bumps erupted over my shoulders. I didn't have fancy lacey bras anymore, and my panties came in a plastic tube. Still, I heard Table's sharp inhale as I bared my body to him. I moved to stand at the end of the bed, naked and fidgeting with self-consciousness. I was not a voluptuous woman, not very big in the breast and ass department. Did he find my thin frame appealing?

If his rigid cock was any indication, he was still ready and waiting for me. As I climbed awkwardly onto the bed, he raised the hand he had been stroking himself with above his head to join the other one.

"You take your time, baby girl. I ain't goin' nowhere. I promise I won't put my hands on you unless you ask. You're in the driver's seat."

I knew he was a man of his word. I straddled him, my wet heat hovering over his stiff cock. He tensed but didn't change his position. I ran my hands over his chest, feeling both the soft skin and the solidity underneath. He was holding back and I knew it was for my sake. He was letting me take over. Letting me lead. Letting me heal. He trusted me with his body. Maybe his heart too?

I explored him, running my hands where I wanted, touching every part of him as he lay there with his eyes on me. I reached between us and wrapped my hand around him. His nostrils flared as he took a sharp breath in, but he didn't move or stop watching. I worked him up and down and he groaned with the effort of holding back. It was a heady feeling to know I could end this, get dressed and walk away, and he wouldn't stop me. Or I could mount him and take what I wanted.

I wanted this. I wanted this so bad I ached for it. I ached for him.

"Feels good, Lori, but you keep it up and I'll be done before you get started," he growled, shifting his hips into my hand.

I let go of him and reached for the foil packet. I saw his jaw clench as I tore it open and rolled the condom over his straining cock. I held him in position as I brought our bodies together, rubbing the head against my wet opening. He was thoroughly coated in my juices when I sank down and allowed him to breach me.

It had been a long time and it hurt. Table was a big man and even though I was ready, taking him wasn't easy. It still felt good as my body opened up. I could see sweat break out over his face and chest as I worked myself down bit by bit, inch by inch, stretching until he was fully inside me. I let out a long, low moan and felt him twitch inside me in response. I rose up and thrust myself down, grinding my hips against him, reveling in the sensation of being so full, so complete.

The last time I had a man inside me was filled with pain and fear. I had been treated as a thing. This time, I was being reborn as a woman.

"Ah—yeah," he grunted, shifting under me, seeking something inside of me. When he found it, I cried out at the thrill of pleasure that shot through me. "Right there, baby, that's it. Fuck yourself on me, Lori. Give me all the beautiful you have in you."

I began working myself up and down his stiff shaft, and he helped by aiming for that spot he'd found. I tried to stifle my cries, but the harder I drove down on him, the louder I got. He was making noises as well. The cords in his neck stood out and his hands wrapped in taut fists as he struggled to keep his promise. My orgasm hit me suddenly and I let out a scream as I lost control and came. My pussy flooded with more wet and I ground down hard as my channel spasmed around him. He choked out a cry and I felt him pulse inside me, finding his own satisfaction.

I couldn't hold myself up any longer and I collapsed on top of him. We were both hot, sweating, and breathing hard. Different and confusing emotions chased their way around my head: joy and sadness, care and fear. My eyes filled with tears as I listened to the steady heartbeat under my ear.

Perfect. Just perfect.

"I promised I wouldn't put my hands on you, Lori, and I still won't, but you gotta know, baby girl, I really want to hold you right now."

More perfect.

"Yes," I managed to gasp before the floodgates opened and I cried. Table was there, his strong arms around me, enfolding me in his secure strength.

"Give it to me, baby. Get it all out, and give it to me," he murmured, and kissed the top of my head. He was still semi-hard inside of me and I was not ready to lose that connection. I burrowed into him, drawing every bit of him I could, clawing at his shoulders and trying to get closer. He took it from me even though I probably hurt him in my frantic grasping.

The deluge finally subsided. I slipped off him, disengaging our bodies and curling in on my side. I heard him leave the bed and go into the bathroom to dispose of the condom. He came right back and slid in behind me, molding himself against me for maximum contact. He placed an arm over my middle and gently stroked his fingers over my ribs. I was grateful he couldn't see my face in the dark; I knew it was swollen and blotchy from crying so hard, and my nose was dripping. He stayed quiet while I sniffed and snatched a tissue up.

"I'm a mess. One big fat ugly mess. I've brought so much trouble to you and your family and I'm so, so sorry. I don't deserve anything from and yet you're going out of your way to help me."

"Hush, baby girl. I don't wanna hear any more 'bout you thinkin' you don't deserve help. Fact of the matter is, there ain't no one out there who needs or deserves it more. You're good to my family and you're good to my daughter. You may be used to having a lot of money, but you ain't afraid to work hard and go without when you need to. I think you know what kind of man I am. There's no way I would have shared my bed with you if I thought you weren't worth the risk. And there is a risk for me, 'cause right now you got a piece of me. It's yours. I'd like to think I got a piece of you and I'll be protectin' and cherishin' that piece with every cell in my body, baby."

His hands stroked over my body as his words settled in my heart. I waited for the urge to run away, but it never came. Instead I placed my hands over his as they trailed over my hip.

"Table, I... I...."

"Hush, baby girl," he repeated. "It's too soon for that, but it will come when the time is right. You get some sleep now. I'll still be here in the morning."

CHAPTER 21

The best? Table was with me every night, holding me in his arms and cuddling close. Each night he made love to me with a tenderness that I would never have expected from a tough biker. His hands, lips, teeth, and tongue touched me in places that I felt through to my soul. I felt loved and treasured by this man who was taking a chance on a broken woman.

The worst? Mostly it was the anticipation of what would come next. Was Jeffrey back in the country and wanting some sort of revenge on me for divorcing him? Even though the papers were done, stamped, and filed, I still didn't feel like it was over. I couldn't say what it was but there was something unfinished.

Table had started doing some work back at the tattoo parlor in town and had looked at moving all three of us into the two-bedroom apartment above the shop. "We can't be living here full-time and startin' a family, baby girl. We'll get us a house soon enough, but the apartment will do for now."

It seemed like Table had already decided my life's new path. The truth was, I didn't mind.

Molly was holding court in the Lair's main room, along with Tambre, Kat, and Eva. Angel was in her customary spot on Betsey's hip. She was in the kitchen making dinner for the gaggle of children that always seemed to surround her.

"'Bout time he got his head outta his ass!"

Tambre was the calm to Molly's fire. "Blue's not dumb. He was just confused and dealing with a lot. It's not every day you have to put your ex-wife in jail."

My ears perked up.

Kat reached for a handful of nuts from the bowl on the coffee table. "You might want to keep it down a bit. His kids are running around down here. You don't want to say anything around them right now about their mom."

I didn't know the whole situation, but from the snippets I'd heard, Blue was Brick and Betsey's son, a local sheriff's deputy, a member of the Dragon Runners, and father to two young children. His ex-wife had been involved in a local drug ring and was now in jail, facing a trial that would most likely put her in prison for a long time. I had been nervous about meeting him, but he had so much going on in his life that my presence was just a blip on his radar. He had no idea who I was and that was fine with me. Blue had been seeing a woman in town who owned a craft store but had been on the fence about making a full commitment to her. Apparently, it had worked out.

Table was shooting pool with Mute and Stud. As if he knew I was watching him, he looked up at me, smiled, and winked. My tummy fluttered and I felt a blush creep over my face as I recalled that same wink as he moved inside me earlier that morning.

"Looks like Blue ain't the only one in love. 'Bout time someone good came along for Table."

I didn't know how to answer that. I shrugged and tried to change the subject.

"So anyone want a refill?"

A chorus of yesses had me reaching for the margarita pitcher.

"None for me, thanks. I'm sticking with water tonight."

This was from Kat, who hadn't said much during Molly's tirade.

The curly-haired woman looked at Mute's wife. "You ain't been drinking nothing but water all day. You want a Coke or something different?"

The shy brunette grinned. "No, thank you. Not too much caffeine and sugar right now."

"What in the Sam Hill— Oh. My. God!" Molly jumped to her feet as she yelled at the top of her lungs and pointed an accusing finger at Kat. "You're pregnant!"

Kat's grin got bigger and she looked toward a now glowering Mute. "Yes, we are."

The screech coming from the kitchen area rang in the rafters as Betsey came barreling into the room. "Oh, my Lord, have mercy! Another grandbaby on the way! Lord, have mercy!" She handed Angel to me so she could hug and cry on the expecting woman.

The conversation turned to due dates, morning sickness remedies, diaper brands, and nursery colors. My attention drifted a little, and I noticed the big biker named Bruiser gesture to Table from the back hallway. Bruiser was a large man with a rounded stomach and thinning hair that was pulled back into a long single curl that barely qualified as a ponytail. Table gave me another glance as he made his way to the mouth of the hallway. Brick was coming down the stairs from the upper floor, and Bruiser gestured to him as well. Both men went down the hall and disappeared from my sight.

Angel grabbed my attention by slapping my mouth with her baby fist and smiling a drooly grin. I made chuffing noises at her while the other ladies continued talking about baby stuff. But my mind was back with Table and hoping for good news.

* * *

"The ladies are occupied for a bit. What didja find?"

Bruiser slurped at his red Solo cup and belched. Table waved a hand in front of his face.

"Jesus, brother! What the hell is in that cup?

Both he and Brick had come back to Bruiser's room. Contrary to his outward slow-moving appearance, the room was neat as a pin and spartan save for a tightly made-up bed and massive computer desk with two giant flat-screen monitors. Several large computer towers were set around the top.

"Red Bull and vodka. Had to have the energy to keep up with all the shit I found."

Table's face grew serious. "How much shit?"

Bruise snorted. "It took me a while. I had to break through a shit ton of firewalls. Them files was hid deep. Some of them sites wasn't exactly on Google, if you know what I mean. But I hit pay dirt. Your senator is into some pretty bad shit. There's stuff here about him makin' deals with a South American arms dealer for bringing in drugs and weapons and we ain't talking legal ones either. Them things is modified for full automatic, beyond military specs. He don't do no sales or nothing, but his big part is cleaning the money. That charity foundation stuff that your girl was involved in? The one that she was supposed to be over in South Africa for? That's what he's been using to launder everything and the proof of it is right'chere on this drive."

Bruiser slurped again and shook his head. "Fuckin' with a kids' charity to hide coke and guns? This guy's been tootin' his horn for years 'bout bein' a big family values' man. What a fuckin' prick."

"What about the son?"

"Oh, he's involved too. From the shit I found out about him, he's followin' in his daddy's footsteps. Got some pics of him here havin' a meetin' at a bar in Columbia."

Bruiser leaned his bulk forward and tapped the wide computer screen. "See this here fella? That's Luis Sanchez. I found him when I dug through to the FBI database. This is one bad dude with the Sanchez drug cartel. I don't have enough time to tell you all the stuff they think this guy's done here in the States, but one thing's for certain, and that's ol' Jeffie-boy here is in it deep. Feds only got a little piece of what's happenin'. We got the rest of the pie."

Table raised an eyebrow as high as he could. "You hacked the FBI?"

Bruiser shrugged, took another slurp of the nasty drink concoction, and burped again. "'T weren't nothin'. I don't mess aroun' none. Just take a quick look-see and get out. I erase my trail real good so we cain't be traced."

"You sure about that?"

"Absolutely positive."

Table wasn't exactly relieved by Bruiser's declaration, but he knew Bruiser was a computer artist. The large man may not be fast-moving or seem to have a lot going on upstairs, but he was a pure genius with a monitor and keyboard.

"Can you track Jeffie-boy now?"

Bruiser shook his head. "He done got off the grid for a spell. I got pics of him whoopin' it up at a cartel party last week, snortin' blow and fuckin' a couple women. I ain't seen him anywhere since, but I cain't find no records or pics of him coming back to the States either. Not even on the private shit his daddy owns. His bank account's been dead for a while now. Credit cards ain't been used here either. He might be on the way, but I cain't tell for sure and don't think he's back yet. 'Sides, I 'spect them rich people cain't be bothered doin' their own dirty work. I'd bet cash money they done hired someone to mess with your girl. Keep her scared and in line."

Table ran a hand over his face and head. "Well Jeffie-boy and Lori are now divorced and that part stayed quiet. I can't understand why he'd still want to mess with her. The only thing I can think of is the Townsend Foundation. I don't see how, since it wasn't her that was launderin' money through it. Fuck, this crap gives me a headache."

"I think it has to do with the trust behind the foundation. Lori, or Vivian, is supposed to control the piece of it her granddaddy left her. I gotta mess of emails that were 'sposed to be from her while she was overseas. They all said proxy voting was gonna be done for her by the Senator. You look back far enough, them emails didn't come from South Africa. They started out at the foundation headquarters and routed through a server over there. The school they been talkin' 'bout? Look at these pics here."

Bruiser clicked on the mouse and two sets of photos came up. One showed a classroom of smiling dark-skinned children wearing uniforms and sitting at desks with open school books. The other showed a grainy image of a falling down shack in a dry, dusty yard.

"This picture is a stock photo from a private school from years back, ain't got nothing to do with the foundation. The other one? That's where the school is supposed to be. 'Parently, that's how Jeffie-boy's father's been cleanin' money and embezzlin' more. Got two sets of books cookin' for the foundation. As long as Lori stayed low, he's been drainin' the accounts. In fact, looks like it's about to go under. Once the FBI finds all this shit, he's gonna need Lori to disappear. And stay that way."

"Fuck."

"You ain't lyin', brother."

Table closed his eyes and let out a long breath as he pinched the bridge of his nose. This was trouble. Bigger trouble than he had ever anticipated. He was part of a simple motorcycle club in western North Carolina that had fought its way to legitimacy and now only wanted to live free and ride free. Yes, the club skirted the law upon occasion and probably always would when needed, but for the most part the men and women of the club worked hard, played hard, and expected to be left alone. In returning to his brothers, he'd brought more than just a battered woman. Drug cartels, illegal arms dealing, and the fuckin' FBI of all things! This was way more than he had a right to ask, but what was the alternative? Take Lori and Angel, and run? How and where? Letting Lori go was not an option. He looked at Brick for answers.

Brick had stayed silent up until that point. "Bruiser, you sure there ain't no way the Feds are going to come knockin' on my door anytime soon?"

Bruiser tipped his cup and snapped a finger against the bottom to dislodge an ice cube. He crunched loudly and a few drops of liquid sprayed when he spoke. "I am ab-so-fuckin-a-loo-telly-one-hunerd-percent positive."

Brick nodded. "The Dragon don't run from trouble, but we don't have to go out guns blazin' neither. Gotta be smart with this shit. Bruiser, I want you to do whatever it is you do, but this time, leave something behind for them Feds to find."

Bruiser wiped the wet specks from his screen. "I told you, bossman. I don't leave nothin' behind. I ain't sloppy like that."

"This time you do. But you leave something behind that points to the senator and all this foundation shit. Some dark site where they find them cooked books or whatever it is you do. Just keep the club and Lori out of it. You've been boastin' about needin' a challenge. Can you do that?"

Bruiser scratched at his scraggly ponytail. "I got some ideas. Yeah, it's a challenge, but I can do it. Good thinking, Brick. Put a bug in the works, lead the Feds to this buttload of evidence, and let them do the work. Club stays out of it. Home free for everyone."

Brick grunted. "Get it done. How long do you think this will take?"

Bruiser shook his head and started pecking at the keyboard with his sausage-shaped fingers. "No way of tellin'. I'll set the trail, but them FBI fellas gotta pick up on it. Might be a coupla days. Might be a week or two. We'll just have to see. If no one picks up, I'll leave a bit more to find, as long as I can still keep us protected."

Table nodded an acknowledgment and left Bruise typing away. He paused at the opening to the great room and just stood there for a moment watching Lori. She was smiling and making noises at Angel.

She fits, he thought. *She fits me, she fits my daughter, she fits my family.*

His focus widened to take in the rest of the group. Mute had Kat securely under his arm and glued to his side. Eva had joined them as well and was curled up on Stud's lap. Cutter was standing behind Molly, absently rubbing her shoulders. Tambre got up to go to her man Taz and greet him with a hug and a kiss. Other members were paired off with their significant others if they had one.

"Nice sight, ain't it?" Brick had come up behind Table as he looked on the group huddled around the couches. "That right there is what we Runners live and die for. If the good Lord took away my sight or my legs or my hands tomorrow and I couldn't put my ass on my bike for the rest of my life, I'd still be happy. I got my family right here and I'd do anything to keep 'em safe. All of 'em. I know you're thinking 'bout the big pile of shit we just found and I feel I need to remind you who we are. We're the Dragon Runners of Bryson City. I'm telling you true, son, we got your back and hers. Ain't nothin' ever gonna change that."

Table felt an unfamiliar tingle hit his nose as he looked at the older man.

Brick wrinkled his nose. "Shit, son! Quit lookin' at me like I'm about to hold your hand and sing 'Kumbaya' to you. Get your ass out there and get your woman."

CHAPTER 22

Time was funny. Sometimes it was your best friend, like on vacation or a leisurely road trip. Other times, it could be the greatest enemy, lurking in the background like a specter ready to pounce. The biggest danger with time? Waiting. Waiting for a phone call, waiting to hear back from a job interview, waiting for a date to arrive, or waiting for a disaster to happen. I wasn't very good at waiting. But the problem with having that waiting time was becoming complacent and relaxed.

It had been several weeks since Bruiser had left a breadcrumb trail for the FBI to discover. And find it they did indeed. The news had been chock full of details behind the new charges brought against Senator Townsend. New discoveries were made daily, and speculation grew about my "demise." It was assumed I was dead and I was okay with that, but Table was worried even more, as now he thought Jeffrey would be more motivated to make it that way.

When so many days passed and nothing happened, we started thinking it was over and Jeffery was gone, probably in hiding from the Columbian cartel. I stopped looking over my shoulder.

Life was good. Table was back at his old job in the tattoo parlor. And I was looking for work. Table was good with me cleaning houses if I wanted to continue that profession, but I was free to do anything I wanted. My degree was in non-profit administration and even though I couldn't use my degree as Vivian Townsend, I still had the knowledge. Maybe there was something else I could do. Perhaps I could find a way to help women who had found themselves in situations similar to mine. I had time.

Too bad I stopped looking over my shoulder.

I was coming out of Psalm's store, Soap-n-Stuff. Angel was in my arms, as well as an array of paper bags holding various soaps, bath bombs, and candles for the home I was making with Table. My thoughts were on what I was going to cook for dinner that night when I spotted Jeffery standing next to an older black SUV out of the corner of my eye, along with another man. I recognized him as one of the senator's former bodyguards.

My blood froze and the bottom dropped out of my stomach. I started to sweat and I felt panic rise in the back of my throat. I had the urge to run but couldn't move.

"Hello, Vivian."

My head exploded with pain and I felt myself falling into blackness.

***

Table was working on the outline of the sugar skull that Bruiser had requested for finding out about Tamara and the custody filing. The trail the large man had traced found that she was in Florida. She had taken up with another biker club and was now one of their club bunnies. She had indeed signed some papers but wasn't anywhere near Raleigh when the custody dispute was originated. Her claim was a man in a black suit came to see her at the bar she was working at and gave her a big bag of cash to sign some papers. She didn't really know what they were, but she needed the money. Custody was never her goal and she was pissed as hell she had to file an affidavit to drop it. Her exact words were: "Don't ever bother me with this shit again, asshole." Bruiser looked but couldn't find a connection back to the foundation, but Table still suspected it was an attempt to fuck things up between him and Lori.

"You find a place yet?"

Table paused to dip more ink. "Not yet. I figure Lori's gonna want somethin' with some land to it for gardenin'. She took to it in Asheville and 'spect she'll want that here. I've got some extra from my fight money, but it's not enough for that."

"Lori, eh? She ain't gonna go back to being Vivian?"

"Nope. Now be still or I'm gonna fuck this up."

"Think she'll stick?"

"Yeah, now quit moving."

"She's a nice girl. Club likes her a lot. Happy for you, brother."

"Thanks, Bruiser. I'm real glad everyone likes her since

she's here to stay. Now if you don't stop squirmin', your skull is gonna look cross-eyed."

Psalm burst into the tattoo shop just as Table's phone rang. She was wild-eyed and gasping for breath.

"Table! He took them! He took them both!"

Table put the tattoo gun down. His brain spiked with sudden adrenaline and his heart went into overdrive. "Say again?"

"Lori came in with Angel a little while ago for some stuff and a quick visit. I was watching when she left and someone was waiting for her outside the store."

Dread and fury built suddenly.

"What happened?"

Psalm bent her slight frame over as air continued to heave in and out of her lungs.

"There were two men. One of them hit her in the head, and the other one grabbed Angel. Lori was knocked out and they put her in the back seat. The other one got in the front and held Angel in his lap. It was a black SUV, but I don't know the make or model. I tried to get to them, but before I got outside, they were gone. It happened so fast. I got part of the license plate and called Blue as I was running over here to tell you. Oh, God, Table!"

Table stripped the latex gloves from his hands. "I guess you can tell I ain't finishin' your outline today, Bruiser. I got a big rat to catch."

Bruiser had already gotten out of the chair with a grunt as he shifted his bulk. "No problem, brother. I'll get my laptop set up. Fucker's got balls to do this in broad daylight.

Anyone else see it happen?"

Psalm had a look of confusion on her face. "Not really. There were some tourists around, but no one took pictures or filmed. It was so quick I don't think other people recognized what was happening. What are you doing?"

Bruiser looked at her as he lifted the fragile-looking machine and pulled up a road map. "'Member that necklace Table gave Lori last week? Got a GPS tracker in it. Thought it might come in handy. See, there's the fucker."

Bruiser pointed to a blinking dot on the screen.

"Does she know?'

Table swiped his phone open and scrolled through his contacts. "Yeah, she does. I ain't startin' off a new relationship by lyin' to my woman. She didn't like it much, but I told her it would give me peace of mind. Seems that was a good call."

He tapped the phone. "Brick? Shit's going down. Time to let the dragon out."

CHAPTER 23

Table eased his way to the front of the dilapidated shack. The other Runners were right behind him, Mute as silent as his name on the right side, and Dodge in between them. They could hear the man inside yelling curses, the crying of a very angry Angel, and the begging sobs of Lori. Table set his eye carefully against one of the cracks in the rotted wood door, and the sight that met his eyes made him grow cold.

Lori was sitting in an old metal folding chair. It was badly bent, and she was having to balance awkwardly in order not to tip over. Angel was in her arms and red-faced as she let her displeasure be known. Lori was jiggling and chuffing at her and trying to get her calmer. Two men were in the room, and Table recognized Jeffrey from the internet photo, but he looked very different from the suave, jet-setting playboy running around with gorgeous models. He was unkempt, his hair sticking out from his head in untamed curls, and his clothes were wrinkled and dirty. The other guy was just as disheveled in a messy black suit and tie. Table guessed this was the bodyguard, and from the dark look on his face, he wanted to be anywhere but there.

"Goddamn cunt! You fucking ruined everything! You should've done what you were told and kept your fucking mouth shut. This is all your fault!"

Jeffrey was agitated and pacing across the floor. A nine millimeter was in his hand and he gestured wildly with his finger hooked in the trigger guard.

"Dad's in jail because of you! All the accounts are frozen. The houses are being watched. All of them! My passport is blocked, and I had to hide and sneak into my own country like I'm some goddamn illegal crossing the border. I'm stuck in this goddamn bumfuck hell-hole because of you and that redneck asshole you've been fucking!"

"Hey, Mr. Townsend, take it easy with the gun."

"You shut the fuck up! If you had done your job, we wouldn't be here right now."

Table saw Brick move in a bit closer on his right side, near the corner of the shack. Stud was right behind him. Everyone was armed, but the shack was old and the condition of the wood wouldn't stop any bullets if Jeffie-boy decided to fire at any of them. They had thought to surround the place, but Table doubted the rotted walls would even slow down any shot and one of his brothers could easily get caught in the crossfire. It would also be a problem in that Lori and Angel were right there in that room. He glanced at Brick, and the older man shook his head. *Not yet.*

"Fucking bitch. Think you can get away from me? You

think a divorce is gonna work? I own you!" Spit flew from his mouth as he screamed into Lori's ear.

He reached out and pressed the gun against her forehead hard enough that Table knew there would be a bruise. Another one to add to her collection of hurts from this piece of shit. His instinct was to rush in and grab both his girls, but that would ensure Lori's death and maybe Angel's. The man was desperate and crazy. Not a good combination.

"Please, Jeffrey, I'm sorry. I'm so sorry. I can make it right if you'll let me. Let's leave now and we can be back in DC by tomorrow and I'll fix it. I promise I'll fix it. We'll leave the baby here for the club to find. Give me my phone back and I'll send one last text and they'll come get her. We'll be long gone and there won't be any reason for them to come after us."

Table could hear the pleading in her voice as she begged to keep Angel safe. She wasn't stupid. She knew if she left with Jeffrey her life would be over in a matter of hours. There was only one way this was going to end.

"You don't get it, you stupid cunt. Your fucking biker gang is the least of my worries. The big bastard you've been spreading your legs for is probably cock-deep in another whore by now. It's the fucking Columbians! When the Feds got that fucking tip about the arms dealing, they seized everything. *All* the warehouses where the guns were stockpiled. It's gone. Every last fucking piece and every last fucking dime! Do you know what that means? Do you, Vivian?"

He pushed the gun harder into her skin, punctuating

his words.

Lori shook her head. Tears were flowing freely down her cheeks. "If it's money, I can pay you back. I can release my trust fund to you. The investments should have made millions by now and I'll give you every penny if we leave now."

The guard tried again. "That isn't a bad idea, Mr. Townsend. A baby would slow things down. We can still get out of here before those bikers find us. Getting her money would make a big difference."

"I said shut the fuck up! You were paid to find her and were supposed to kill her and make it look like an accident."

"Your father didn't think it was a good idea to have her killed just yet. He only wanted her scared and isolated, kept on the move because he might still need her for the foundation."

"Fuck my father! You see where that bastard is sitting now don't you? It was his bright idea to stage the custody fight with the ex-wife, like that would fucking do anything. I know he had in mind to scapegoat Vivian for the foundation accounts, but what about the goddamn guns? Yeah, he's fucking brilliant!"

"The senator thought it best to keep her alive as long as he could keep the foundation running. His orders were to keep her alone and running."

"Yeah, you did a fucking great job with that, didn't you? Like you think fucking up some farm equipment or leaving a goddamn scarf was supposed to do the trick. You fucked up with her van brakes bad enough, she should've died then.

You're not paid to think, you fucking idiot."

The guard had finally had enough. "I'm done with this shit show."

He barely got the words out before Jeffrey took the gun from Lori and shot him. The guard's head flew back as bright red sprayed the wall behind him. Lori let out a short cry and clutched the screaming Angel closer.

Table could see the perfect purpling circle on Lori's forehead. Brick did too.

"So fucking stupid, you bitch! I have a goddamn price on my head. The Feds will put me in jail alongside Daddy. The goddamn Columbians will kill us. Daddy told me to lay low in Rio, but then that goddamn photo came up on social media and all the fucking questions from the press about you." He waved the gun around and spoke in a singsong mocking voice. "Where is Mrs. Townsend? What happened to her? Are the rumors true and she was really a victim of domestic abuse?" He pointed the gun back at her. "Shut that goddamn kid up before I do!"

Table's fury level jumped to level ten. Only Brick's restraining hand kept in from rushing into the shack. He could hear Lori's pleading through the red haze that filled his vision.

"Please don't hurt her, Jeffrey! She's only a baby!"

"Fucking press. Fucking Columbians. Fucking bikers. And that fucking bodyguard that let you go. I told him to kill you while you were in West Virginia. We were gonna put out a story about you dying of a fever in Africa. Instead, that fucker gave you money and let you escape. Apparently he had a soft spot for whores. He won't be making that mistake again."

The man paced again, growing more and more agitated. Table knew it wouldn't be long before he blew.

"One big fat fucking goddamn mess, and you think you can give me a few million dollars and walk away scot-free? Stupid, stupid, stupid!"

He swung the gun wildly and connected with Lori's temple. Blood flew as she cried out and crashed to the floor, protecting Angel with her body by taking the impact on her shoulder. He reared back a leg to kick her while she was down. Lori curled up into a protective ball around Angel, ready to take whatever blow came her way.

Table couldn't hold back anymore. He couldn't watch as his woman took more abuse while protecting his child.

"Hey, Jeffie-boy? Big-talkin' guy when you can beat up on a woman smaller and weaker than you. How 'bout you find your balls and be a fuckin' man for a change? Come out here and face me, motherfucker!"

Jeffrey was startled enough at the discovery he had an audience he forgot about Lori and started firing the gun randomly at the walls, sending shots through the thin material. The Dragon Runner returned fire. Bullets flew back at him from all sides, striking the deranged man in the chest and torso. Wood splinters rained down on Lori as she covered the baby with her body.

Table burst through the door as he heard Brick yell, "Hold your fire!" Jeffrey's look was a combination of surprise and fear as Table rushed him. He drew back his fist and let loose a roundhouse punch, and Jeffrey's head snapped hard to the side. The gun went off again as he fell to the ground, out cold.

Just like that it was over.

Table hit the dirt where Lori still hovered over Angel's screaming body. "I got you, baby girl. I got you."

Brick took over. "Mute, text Betsey that we got 'em and be ready. Dodge, get the truck and the first aid kit. We're gonna need them ASAP."

Lori finally lifted her streaked face and stood up, burying herself into Table's body, clutching and crying. Angel was still screaming, but the moment she felt her daddy, her angry cries diminished into fussy whimpers.

"I got you, baby girl. Both my baby girls." Table cradled the two females in his care as he repeated the words over and over. "I got you. I got you. Always, Lori."

A strange burn started in his chest. It felt cold and hot at the same time. A wave of dizziness hit his head and he couldn't hold himself up anymore. The floor came up to meet his body as crumbled to the ground.

"Table, oh my God, Table!"

His eyes were glazed with pain as he reached up a hand to stroke softly over her cheek. He gazed with fading eyes at the streak of crimson his fingers left behind.

"Love you, baby girl. It's worth it, I promise. Take care of my Angel."

"I love you, too! Please don't leave me, Table!"

"Love you, Lori."

"Stay with me, please!"

"Love you."
He stopped breathing.

CHAPTER 24

Table was gone. In the chaos that ensued after the short battle, Brick and some of the other bikers took him somewhere and Stud took me and Angel back to the Lair. I felt as if my heart had been ripped from my body and all that was left was a shell of the person I had become. The woman Table had loved enough to die for. My fragile life meant nothing now that I was by myself again.

I stayed in the bed in Table's Lair room, smelling his scent on the sheets and keeping his pillow wet with my tears. I could hear other club people moving around in the main room. Two other members had some minor injuries and were being fussed over. Betsey came in with Angel attached to her hip and badgered me into taking a shower to get the blood off me. She stood over me and made me eat something, but it all tasted like cardboard and ashes. I was numb. A body with no purpose or drive.

But I had to get it together. I still had Angel. My precious Angel, who was now the only part of Table I had left. She needed me more than ever and I needed her just as much. I held and played with her while surrounded by Table's family. Both of us would have to work through our grief.

Maybe I could find work in town and pay the rent on the apartment we had moved into as a family. It would be rough, because that's where Table and I had been planning on starting a life together, but for Angel's sake I would do it. I tried to talk to Betsey about it several times but she kept blowing me off with a flip of her hand and a *pshhht* through her red lips.

"Ain't no hurry. It's all gonna work out just fine. Just wait for Brick to come home."

It was late when Brick and the others came back. I was holding Angel in the living area and listening to Betsey and the other club ladies talk about labor and delivery when he came into the room. His face was long and tired, and he looked every bit his age, but he still had a commanding air around him.

"Lori, got a minute?"

I nodded and handed Angel to Betsey.

"You get some food in you and the baby?"

"Yes, we did. Thank you."

The serious look on his face prompted me to silence.

"In a little while, you and I are gonna take a little ride. I got something I need to show you and you're gonna need to put it in your brain and keep it there. It don't get said. Never. Not in this lifetime or the next. The safety of this club depends on it and I wouldn't be doing this unless I knew I could trust you with it. You get me?"

These people had accepted me without question into the family fold. It was an easy decision.

"I'll do whatever I need to do. I'm so grateful to you and the club for all your help. I promise I'll pay you back as soon as I can."

"Ain't no payback for family. Table made you a part of us and that's the way it is."

"Does that matter now since Table—since he's—" My throat closed up, denying me to say the words aloud.

Brick glanced at a confused Betsey and then back at me. "Lori, do you think Table's dead?"

My heart jumped into high gear. "Brick?"

The older man shook his head. "Darlin, Table's over at the doc's place. He was losin' too much blood, and we had to get him there quick. I thought you knew. I ain't gonna lie to ya, he ain't outta danger, but he's still here. Mute had to do CPR and breathe for him for a bit on the way, and Doc had to do some quick work, but he's still alive and wants to see you. It ain't pretty. Can you handle it?"

Less than half an hour later, I found myself sitting behind Brick on a fat cruising bike, heading up the twisting, turning road known as the Tail of the Dragon. I had learned that being on the back of a bike made a statement about the people riding, but Betsey said it didn't matter for this particular occasion.

Brick pulled off the main road at some point onto what amounted to a long gravel driveway. He parked the bike near a yellow-and-white prefab house surrounded by woods. A matching two-car garage was nearby, as well as an above ground pool with a fountain spouting into the air surrounded by a redwood deck with lot of lounge chairs and a covered hot tub. This was clearly someone's vacation getaway spot.

Brick let me dismount the bike first before backing it into a spot next to two others. As we mounted the short steps to the porch, the door opened and an older man stepped out and jerked his head in greeting.

"Brick. Nice to see you. This her?"

"Yeah. Doc Holbrook, meet Lori Matthews."

The doctor stretched out a hand and pumped mine twice. "Nice ta meetcha."

He turned back to Brick. "We got at least another week or two 'fore he can be moved. Damn lucky to be here. Come on in."

Brick looked at me as the doctor shuffled back into the house. "Remember, Lori. Not a word. I'll explain why later."

The sight that met my eyes shook me to my core. My knees lost their strength and Brick caught me before I hit the floor. In the middle of the living room was a hospital bed surrounded by an IV stand and two blinking monitors. Table was propped up in the bed, the covers at his waist revealing white gauze covering the right side of his chest. He looked pale, his face drawn with exhaustion. Even his tattoos looked faded, but he was alive and breathing.

"Hey, baby girl."

His tone was tired and weak, but it was the best sound I'd ever heard in my life. He raised his arm that was free of tubes and beckoned to me.

"Come over here and give me some sugar."

I nearly stumbled in my haste to get to him. Tears blinded me as I leaned into him, careful not to disturb the medical dressing. He kissed me lightly and pulled me into the bed next to him, tucking me close to his good side.

Brick sat down heavily in one of the armchairs close to the bed. "Lung shot and gut shot. Died once while Doc was workin' on him 'n had to use the fancy paddle to shock 'im back. We couldn't take him to a hospital under the circumstances 'cause they gotta report any gunshot wounds to the police. That would put the club in the spotlight and open up a whole can of worms 'bout how it happened, who did it, and all that shit. Doc Holbrook ain't no stranger to the club and we have this place set up for this kind of thing. Ain't happen often, but if it does, we're ready for it. I'm sorry you didn't know 'bout him not being dead. I suppose with all the shit goin' down, none of us thought to tell you and just assumed you knew. Almost became a fact, but he's a stubborn cuss when it comes to takin' care of you and his little girl. He's still gotta stay here a mite longer 'til he gets healed."

Table's heartbeat was strong and steady under my cheek and he held me close, stroking my arm with his fingertips. Brick kept talking.

"I have an idea for you, if you wanna hear it. Bruiser's got a lot of stuff he can do with all his computer shit. He can you set up with a legit ID, social security number, driver's license an' all that kinda stuff. He can also set up the death of Vivian Townsend so you ain't got no binding to that life. You just say the word and he'll make it happen."

I swallowed. "How would I die?"

"Same as what them other assholes had planned. Fever. Bruiser's fixin' up a medical record for you for the Feds to find. Made it that you died from it and was cremated in Africa. Ashes scattered round the grounds of the school. He found the plan for it somewhere in the files he hacked from the Senator. 'Parently, they were gonna put that shit out after they pinned the money fraud shit on you. We just changed the dates to just after the Senator got arrested. Made it look recent. File's gonna say 'natural causes', but I bet my last dollar, there's people out there gonna think different. Don't really matter none. You need to think on it some?"

It was strange hearing about my death. It was more like I was hearing about a stranger who died on foreign soil and not me. "Please tell Bruiser to go ahead."

What happened to Jeffrey?

The question ran through my head and stayed there. I knew it was best for me not to ask it out loud. I already knew the answer. He wasn't coming back.

"How's Angel doing? I'm missin' both my girls." Table kept his soothing touch over my skin.

"She's good. I'm sure she wants her daddy back, but she's getting very comfortable having Betsey play grandmother."

He chuckled and then grimaced in pain.

"Fuck, I can't wait to get outta this bed and back where I need to be."

"Ain't no hurry. Tattoo shop'll still be there when you're on your feet again. Doc says it's gonna be a while before you're all the way healed. You got time." Brick heaved himself out of the chair as he spoke. "We need to be gettin' back to the Lair. I got stuff that needs doin'. I'll give you a few more minutes and then we need to hit the road. We'll be back in a few days and maybe bring the baby with."

I didn't want to leave, but Doc's place didn't look like it was set up to receive guests, and it would have been too presumptuous to ask if I could stay. Table seemed to understand. "It's okay, Lori. You can come see me in a few days, and I should be back at the Lair real soon."

I wiped my eyes and looked at Brick. "It seems inadequate to just say thank you for everything. You've given me my life back."

The older man nodded. "That's plenty. You just take care of my boy and his little girl, and remember the people that have helped you in case you get a chance to help back someday."

He left the room and I was alone with Table. Tears started pricking my eyes again. "I'm so, so sorry for all the hurt I've caused you. I can't—I can't—"

"Hush now, Lori, none of this is your fault. You didn't start this shit so don't you own it. It's over and I would do the same thing again if I had too. The only thing I wish I could change anything was where I got shot. That son of a bitch hurt like a mother."

I giggled while tears ran down my face. "Now what?"

"Now we wait for me to get my ass outta this bed and start our lives. Bruiser took care of the Feds and there ain't nothin' to lead them to us or the club. I got some money in the bank. Not much, but enough to get us through the next month or two until I can get back to work. We still got us a place to live and I've already laid claim to you so you'll be wearing my patch and stayin' by my side every night. I know you've been used to having a lot, but I'm bankin' on you wantin' somethin' else other than a fancy house and car. I'm hopin' you'll be willin' to give up all of that mess and take on a broken man and his daughter. 'Specially since that man loves every cell in your body and would fight to keep you with him." He grinned at me. "If love don't work, I got some great guilt trip material."

"That's not funny." I tried to sound serious even though I smiled at his joke.

"Maybe not but it's true. I love you, Lori. You said to Brick that 'thank you' was inadequate to how you were feeling 'bout him and the club. I think the same 'cause those three words will never come up to what I feel for you and I'll bleed my last drop to keep you and Angel safe. My biggest fear is that while I'm laid up in this bed, you'll get the urge to run and this time I can't stop you."

"I'm not running anymore, Table. I've found where I belong and I have no plans to give it up."

He seemed to relax at my words. His eyes fluttered closed as he gave a long sigh and I knew he was getting tired. He still had a long way to go in his recovery, but my man was a fighter. We would be okay.

Bruiser met me at the door when Brick and I got back to the Lair and handed me a bunch of printed papers.

"Don't ask me how I did all this, just know it's done."

The papers were the new me. I was now officially Lori

Matthews with ID, driver's license, birth certificate, and even a social security number. Joy burst in me as I realized Vivian Townsend was truly gone and in her place was a new life. Mine.

EPILOGUE

EIGHT MONTHS LATER

Table looked at the clock on the wall and switched the XM radio from AC/DC to a different station. The buzz of tattoo needles filled the air along with a Sesame Street sing-along CD.

The wheels on the bus go round and round.

Round and round.

Round and round.

The man in the station chair visibly gritted his teeth against the noise. "What the fuck, dude? Change it back, man!"

Table didn't look up from his work. "Can't do that for about ten minutes or so."

"Ten minutes? Who the fuck is in charge here?"

The bell over the shop door tinkled and a pink-dress-clad body wobbled in and made a beeline for Table.

"DaDaDaDa."

Table wiped the extra ink from the man's skin and set

the needles to the side just in time to catch the blabbering toddler up in his arms as he stood. "This is who is in charge. Watch your mouth around my daughter."

The man with the half-finished tattoo just stared as Table landed a bunch of loud smooches all over the giggling child's face. "Who's Daddy's best girl? Who is it? Is it Angel?"

A small woman in a short denim skirt and white blouse walked in after the little girl. Her shoulder-length blonde hair had the remnants of black dye at the tips and she wore a vest that had the Dragon Runners MC emblem on the back along with the words "property of." A giant purse was over one shoulder and a handful of shopping bags were in the other. Table greeted her with a long, warm kiss. "How's my other best girl?"

"Ready to drop. We did a big Costco run this morning for Betsey and spent the rest of the day up at the Lair helping her with plans for the newest club acquisition. That motel over in Maggie Valley is going to be great once we get it back to where it needs to be. I'm thinking takeout for dinner tonight."

"Sounds good to me, baby girl. You get the mail?"

She pulled out a handful of different-sized envelopes from her purse and plopped them on the counter. "I haven't gone through it yet, but I expect it's the usual assortment of bills and junk mail. I saw where Publisher's Clearing House says I won a million dollars in their sweepstakes. Wouldn't that be nice?"

Table chuckled and smacked his lips against her forehead. "If only. Can't complain too loud though. We have enough to pay our bills at least and the shop is in the black. Even if we don't have much extra, it will come soon enough." He went to the counter and shuffled through the stack of mail while humming the children's tune. The little girl put her head on her father's shoulder and stuck a finger in her mouth.

"Did you hear from your cousin about the farm?"

"Yeah, he's settled in permanent and working the garden. Harvest was huge this past summer and fall. He's looking to open up the other fields that ain't been used in a long time. With all the push about people wantin' more organic stuff, he thinks he can turn a bigger profit and really bring the farm back to what it once was. The Bobbsey twins are tickled pink about the upturn. Martha's been going out with this Floyd guy and Carol's been—"

"Hey, you gonna finish this?"

Table ignored the impatient voice of the customer and pulled out a plain white envelope. "In a minute, buddy. Lori? Did you see this one?"

Lori looked up from where she had started sweeping. "No, what is it?"

Table handed her the envelope with a somber look on his face. The address was the tattoo shop, but the first line read, "To the family of Vivian Townsend."

Lori held it like she would a snake.

"Open it, baby girl."

"I can't."

"It's okay, Lori. Months okay. You're sleepin' easy now. Ain't nothin' here gonna change that. Open it."

Lori's hand shook as she ran a finger under the seal of

the envelope. She pulled out a single sheet of paper and took a deep breath while scanning it. Her face crumpled and she pressed a hand to her mouth to suppress a sob that tried to come out. Table's gut clenched in response.

"What is it?"

"I've— I'm—"

"Spit it out, Lori."

She took a calming breath. "Lori Matthews has been named the sole beneficiary of Vivian Townsend's estate. The trust and everything else I—she owned herself. My— her lawyer fixed this somehow so I get the lot of it."

"What does that mean?"

She looked up at Table with shining eyes. "It means we don't need to claim any sweepstakes anytime soon."

Table's jaw tightened a bit. "Congratulations."

"What's wrong?"

"Nothin'."

"Tell me."

"Nothin'."

"Table, please talk to me."

"Do I have to spell it out?"

"Yes, you do."

"Fu—udgecicles!"

"Dud-tah!" Angel's head popped up from her father's shoulder, suddenly awake at the thought of the cold treat.

Table put the child down. "Back in the freezer, Angel cakes."

"Hey! I'm still waiting!" The yell from the customer followed them as they made their way to the break room.

Table pulled out the ice cream and tore the wrapper off before handing it to the excited toddler.

"Talk to me, Table. This is good news, right?"

"You're rich again, aren't you? You can go back to your old life jet-setting and doin' all that sh— stuff you used to do that I can't give you here in Podunk, NC."

Lori blinked. "For a smart man, you can be incredibly stupid sometimes. Did you not hear me? *We* don't need any sweepstakes prize. *We* have extra now. *We* can pay off the last of the medical bills and what other debts *we* have."

She turned to face Table, her eyes snapping fire. "I've been rich. Bought anything I wanted anytime I wanted it, sometimes just because I could. But I can't buy what I have now."

She tore open one of the shopping bags and began to rummage through it. "I have the Dragon Runners family and the friendship of some of the strongest women I've ever met. True friendship. Not one where everyone wants to know you for your name and connections."

Angel dropped a bit of ice cream and left a huge streak of chocolate down the front of her pink dress.

"I get to spend every day with a precious little girl I love like she was my own. She's calling me 'mama' and that is priceless."

Lori moved to stand in front of Table. "And I found the absolute love of my life in a man who was willing to die for me. I'd rather be struggling by his side for a lifetime than getting my nails done weekly at an overpriced day spa salon." She handed him a blue and pink box. "And if what

I suspect is true, in another six months I'll have another reason to love you."

Angel had lost interest in the treat and had placed the melting ice-cream bar on the floor. She danced around her father's legs to the Itsy Bitsy Spider song that played over the shop's speakers. Table's watering eyes barely glanced at the pregnancy test in his palm. "I'm gonna be a daddy again."

"Dadeeee!" the toddler sang out.

"Yes, you are. And now we can afford to get a bigger place. One that has lots of space that we can fill with more children. You're the best father I know and every day I love you even more for it."

Table sniffed and ran a hand over his smooth head. His heart was ready to burst. "You know somethin'? After Tamara, I never thought I'd love someone again. Turns out, I never loved that woman, 'cause what I felt for her don't come close to what I feel for you. She wore my patch and my ring. You're only wearing my patch now. I want you to wear my ring."

He watched as Lori's eyes teared up to match his own. "It would be the greatest honor in my life."

"Kiss her already, dude! I got to be at work in an hour and this thing's only half done."

The yell from the customer broke the moment. Angel tried to pick up the ice cream stick and abruptly sat in the puddle of melted chocolate, further staining her dress. Table bit back a swear word and picked her up, holding her at arm's length to avoid smearing the mess on his clothes.

Lori let out a watery laugh and took the child from him. "I'll take her upstairs and get her cleaned up. Dinner in an hour? I'll call something in at the deli and you can pick it up when you're finished here."

"Yeah. You sure you want more of these hooligans runnin' around?"

"Absolutely."

Lori gathered a few of the bags in one hand as she balanced the sticky little girl on the other, not minding the shared chocolate on her shirt. She was at the steps that led to the upper rooms when Table stopped her.

"Hey, Lori?"

She turned, and Table was struck by how perfect the picture looked.

"Love you, baby girl."

Her smile was blinding and Table lost his breath.

"Love you too."

CONNIE'S WORDS

Chingada: expletive meaning "holy shit!" or
"oh fuck!"
Chica: girl or young woman
Gringa: Foreigner
Pendejos: stupid or asshole
Mi hermana: my sister

EVA'S WORDS

Mo rún: My love

Thanks for reading *Table,* Dragon Runner MC, book four. I do hope you enjoyed Table and Lori's story. I appreciate your help in spreading the word, including telling a friend. Before you go, it would mean so much to me if you would take a few minutes to write a review and share how you feel about my story so others may find my work. Reviews really do help readers find books. Please leave a review on your favorite book site.

Don't miss out on New Releases, Exclusive Giveaways and much more!

LIKE ME ON FACEBOOK:
WWW.FACEBOOK.COM/AUTHORMLNYSTROM/
FOLLOW ME ON TWITTER:
WWW.TWITTER.COM/ML_NYSTROM
FOLLOW ME ON GOODREADS:
WWW.GOODREADS.COM/AUTHOR/
SHOW/17103715.M_L_NYSTROM
VISIT MY WEBSITE FOR MY CURRENT BOOKLIST:
WWW.MLNYSTROM.COM

I'd love to hear from you directly, too. Please feel free to email me at www.mlnystrom.com/contact or check out my website /www.mlnystrom.com/ for updates.

ACKNOWLEDGMENTS

Table was not really on the horizon to be a book until someone who read *Stud*, book two, fell in love with him, and said he needed a story. Since he had a lot of integrity, was a strong caring man, and had just become a father, I decided he needed to be a protector. Who better to protect than a woman dealing with past victimhood and was struggling to overcome her fears and get her life back on track? The statistics on domestic abuse are staggering and my heart goes out to the women, men, and children who are living in those nightmare situations. Please consider donating to local shelters and other programs as they provide help and resources for people trying to get their lives back.

A big thanks goes out to all who helped me put this book together. Olivia Ventura, Barbara Hoover, Brittany Alexander, Casey Ford, Franci Neill, Sue Griffiths, Robert Holland, Kim Deister, all of you rock! Becky Johnson, and the rest of the crew at Hot Tree Publishing, I can't thank you enough for your support and guidance. Love you, ladies!

ABOUT THE PUBLISHER

Hot Tree Publishing opened its doors in 2015 with an aspiration to bring quality fiction to the world of readers. With the initial focus on romance and a wide spread of romance subgenres, Hot Tree Publishing have since opened their first imprint, Tangled Tree Publishing, specializing in crime, mystery, suspense, and thriller.

Firmly seated in the industry as a leading editing provider to independent authors and small publishing houses, Hot Tree Publishing is the sister company to Hot Tree Editing, founded in 2012. Having established in-house editing and promotions, plus having a well-respected market presence, Hot Tree Publishing endeavors to be a leader in bringing quality stories to the world of readers.

Interested in discovering more amazing reads brought to you by Hot Tree Publishing? Head over to the website for information:

WWW.HOTTREEPUBLISHING.COM